CURSE OF A WINTER MOON

ALSO BY MARY CASANOVA

Stealing Thunder
Wolf Shadows
Riot
Moose Tracks

CURSE OF A WINTER MOON

MARY CASANOVA

HYPERION BOOKS FOR CHILDREN
New York

Printed in the United States of America

First Edition
3 5 7 9 10 8 6 4 2

The text for this book is set in 12.5-point Garamond 3.
ISBN 0-7868-0547-1
ISBN 0-7868-2475-1 (lib.bdg.)

Library of Congress Cataloging-in-Publication Data on file

To those who shine a light
in the darkness

With deep gratitude, I wish to acknowledge the many individuals who have left their fingerprints on this book. From reference desk librarians to scholars found via the Internet, from writers and teachers to friends and family—without their hearts and minds, this book truly would not have been possible.

In particular, I wish to thank editors Donna Bray and Julia Richardson; my agent, Kendra Marcus; Tamara Griggs at Princeton University for her historical critique and comments; Barb Santucci, Jane Resh Thomas, Cindy Rogers, Karen Severson, Lynn Naeckel, Sue Commerford, and Sheryl Peterson; the Aitken family, who read an early draft by firelight at their cabin; Connie Lacker, my assistant; my teenage children, Katie and Eric, for their honesty, support, and willingness to read my work in its early stages; Christine Charles, our French exchange student; Grandpa Max, who "held down the fort" so I could go to France for research; and finally, to Charles, my husband and photographer, who traveled with me to Provence—to explore its landscape and complex history—and back again. *Merci beaucoup!*

BIRTH TO GRAVE

SOUTHERN FRANCE
December 24, 1553

All night, the Mistral wind blew down from the Alps, damp and chill, and howled through cracks, despite windows shuttered tight against December. At the start of my mother's birth pangs, Papa had fetched the midwife, who bustled into our one-room dwelling. She joined Madame Troubène at my mother's bedside, then sent me and Papa downstairs.

In my father's smithy, I lay before the fire wishing there was something I could do. Through the overhead floorboards, my mother's cries rose and fell, quieted for a time, then came again. I wanted to help, to get her a drink of water. Instead, I waited for the midwife to leave.

Sometime during that long night I drifted off to sleep and my father must have carried me upstairs to my straw-filled mattress. Before dawn, I awoke.

In the amber light of the hearth's blazing fire, in the

room's only chair, sat Madame Troubène. She looked so tired that I hardly recognized her, my mother's nanny, like a grandmother to me. Lines crossed her forehead and tugged at the corners of her gray eyes and mouth.

"Marius," she whispered, inviting me closer with a curve of her finger. "Kiss your brother." In her arms she cradled a tiny bundle.

Barefooted, I jumped up—strewn rushes protected me from the icy wooden floor—and came nose-to-nose with a sweet-smelling face, red as a ripe apple. The nose, eyes, and lips—everything—were tiny and perfect. "Wh-what's his name?" I asked.

"Jean-Pierre," she said, her voice guarded.

I smiled at my new brother and touched my forefinger to his nose. Madame Troubène pulled the blanket back from the baby until he squirmed and cried like a lamb. Only then did I remember it was Christmas Eve; soon the villagers would follow the cart with the lamb to church to celebrate Christmas Day.

"Poor one, this one," Madame Troubène said, gently caressing the baby's soft cheeks. "The mark is upon him."

"What mark?" I studied my little brother's body, pink and wrinkled as a newborn mouse. I breathed in his scent—sweet as lavender fields in bloom—but saw no mark.

She paused, chewed on her wrinkled lips, then spoke. "Why . . . the mark, the curse . . . of the *loup garou*, the werewolf, to be sure." She lifted her fingers to her forehead and made the sign of the cross over her chest.

I stared at the baby.

"Everyone knows that a child born on Christmas Eve is

cursed," she said. "Only God knows what will become of this one."

My stomach tightened. I inched back from the baby. The *loup garou*? Only a short time past, I had helped Madame Troubène bury a wolf's foot outside the village walls to keep away such evil.

Suddenly, I longed for my mother, her arms open, ready to draw me close. From somewhere outside, a rooster began to crow. "I want to see my mama," I said, starting boldly for her bed in the shadowed corner.

Madame Troubène's arm stopped me like a thick branch. She was short but solid. With her other arm, she held the baby close against her chest. She kissed the top of the baby's head, and then, through tears, she slowly shook her head. "Your mother is gone."

I stared at my parents' empty bed.

"Her strength," she said, "faded . . . vanished moments after your brother was born. She died, Marius."

My body stiffened. Death meant bodies carted off through village streets, sometimes piled outside the walls until they could be buried. Death meant burnings at the stake or bodies hanging, toes purple and cold. I had touched the bare foot of a hanging man, just once, colder than anything I'd ever felt. Crows pecked flesh clean from the skeletons. Then, and only then, were the bodies—what was left of them—removed from the village. I shuddered. Refused to believe my mother could be dead.

"Where's Papa?" I demanded, fists tight against my sleep shirt. I began to shiver uncontrollably. "I want my papa," I demanded. "I want to see my mama."

Wind rattled a shutter, then blew it open, and pale

light fell into the room. Low in the distant sky, the moon hung like a halo over Venyre. Madame Troubène rose with the baby and hurried to the window. "I will care for you," she said. "You and your papa and little Jean-Pierre." Then she closed the shutters.

Tears came, blurring everything. I wanted my mother. I wanted to hear the sweet sound of her lute, which she strummed every evening as I drifted to sleep. I wanted to watch her braid and coil her hair, to feel her fingertips gently tickle my sides until I filled with laughter. I dropped to the mattress, buried myself beneath the wool blanket, and began to wail.

Madame Troubène's voice came, raised more loudly than my own. "I wouldn't put this burden on you," she said, her voice breaking, "but your poor mother's last words . . . she made me promise I'd tell you. . . ."

Curled beneath the scratchy blanket, tight as a clam in its shell, I stopped crying long enough to listen, my breath trapped in my throat.

"She said, 'Tell Marius to take good care of his brother.'"

THE VILLAGE

SIX YEARS LATER
December 12, 1559

I raced down Venyre's narrow and winding dirt streets, searching for my brother, Jean-Pierre. One moment he was right at my side, and the next he had vanished. Rounding a corner too quickly, I tripped over a woman huddled near a basket, and fell.

Below the edge of my wool breeches, my knees were scraped red and I wanted to curse, but my mother had taught me to show charity to everyone. "Sorry," I mumbled, picking myself up from the ground.

The woman, who was forever cross-eyed, huffed and lifted the edge of her mud-crusted skirt, checking her hem and revealing layers of underskirts and petticoats. She wagged her finger. "Kill my chickens and you'll have to buy them!" At her feet, five chickens clucked nervously in a round woven cage, which the woman picked up by its handle. She walked away, grumbling, ". . . barely survive as it is." Then she called out, "Chickens! Plump chickens!"

I walked briskly through the square, filled with midday activity, where a crowd formed around a caravan of merchants setting up their wares. Perhaps my brother was there. This was the third time he'd vanished in a week. His sudden disappearances caused me worry, especially with the approach of Christmas Eve.

"Goods from the Far East!" called one merchant. "China, silks, the finest spices!"

More and more, the streets and shops of Venyre were filled with goods made beyond the village. Villagers traded olive oil, wool, and wine for strange things, new things. I searched the crowd for a waist-high boy, dark hair cropped above his eyes.

"Italian pottery!"

With a sideways glance—I had no need for fancy bowls or expensive spices—I passed merchant stands and walked up rue des Fleurs, a narrow street shaded by two-story houses and shops built tightly side by side. In the shade, the air grew chilly and I shivered.

Though my hair, like my father's, covered the nape of my neck and was tied back with a leather string, I pulled my cap—wool-thrummed with gray tufts like down from a bird's nest—over my ears. My jerkin, shoulders tufted, hung to midthigh; I wore it over two wool shirts and belted it with a cord. I was glad I wasn't like some, struggling to get through winter in threadbare clothes. Each year, my father bought me and Jean-Pierre a new set of garments.

Outside a tavern, in a patch of sunlight, two soldiers were laughing. They sported knee-high leather boots with overhanging cuffs and silver buckles.

I glanced at my simple leather shoes and hurried on. Other boys my age were working as apprentices, learning artisans' trades as silversmiths, woodcarvers, cobblers, potters, weavers. . . . At twelve, I was well past the age at which I should have begun to learn a trade. Most boys followed in their father's footsteps. Everyone respected and needed the skills of the blacksmith; it could be a good trade for me. Someday I'd be more than my brother's nursemaid.

Pigeons pecked at crumbs outside the mill owned by Seigneur Beaumont, where most village women bought flour and baked their bread. The smell of baked goods met my nose; I breathed in deeply, could almost taste the fresh, warm loaves. But I kept walking.

I headed toward the wide wooden door of my father's blacksmith shop and closed it behind me. Like fog, smoke hung thick in the smithy. My father was pounding at his anvil, his muscles hard and strained as those of a working ox. Coals glimmered red in the forge.

He looked up with probing dark eyes. A slight smile passed across his bearded face, the way sun peeks through heavy clouds and disappears again. "Marius," he said.

Arms at my sides, I clenched my hands into fists. "Have you seen Jean-Pierre?"

Face smeared with soot, skin flushed and sweat-beaded, my father shook his head. "No, Marius. He's your responsibility."

I was tired beyond words of this reminder. "But Madame Troubène can care for Jean-Pierre. I should start working here, with you."

"She's as old as a tortoise," Papa said. "She can barely

7

rise from her bed every morning as it is. Soon, we'll be caring for her, not the other way around. Your brother needs you. Some would harm him, you realize."

"Yes," I replied wearily. Only last year, I had watched soldiers drag two women to the stake to be burned as witches. If someday the villagers became convinced that Jean-Pierre was truly a *loup garou* . . . I clamped my arms tightly over my chest and exhaled heavily. If only the midwife had been willing to say that Jean-Pierre was born on Christmas Day, things might have been different; but she prided herself on being a "godly woman" who always spoke the truth. Moments after my brother was born, she must have told the whole village of his Christmas Eve birth. Certainly, my father's words were true, but putting the burden of my brother's safety on me wasn't fair.

"I've heard talk," I said, "but that doesn't mean anyone would actually harm him. He's only a child. Even if he were—"

"No, don't say it," my father scolded. He glanced toward the door.

My chest grew tight with resentment, tight with holding back all the things I wished I could say to my father. "All you care about is Jean-Pierre," I blurted, daring to show my real feelings. "What about *my* apprenticeship?"

With a slight shifting of my feet, I drew back, even though I knew my father wouldn't beat me, not like many fathers who regularly reminded their children of their place. Still, I couldn't stop myself. "Doesn't my well-being matter at all to you?"

My father studied me, seemed to look through me to somewhere far beyond. One hand went to his beard, which he kept shorter than most men's so it wouldn't catch fire, and he grasped his chin.

I waited for a reaction, *wanted* a reaction. Even if he swung at me, that would be better than the distance he kept.

Finally, he spoke. "It's not that simple," he said, meeting my eyes, as if he wanted to say more.

I hoped he would continue, but he returned to pounding at the anvil. A flurry of sparks flew in the dim light. Leaning hard against the door, I stared beyond him at the fire. At that moment, I hated him and the way he was beyond my reach. "That's all, then?" I asked, my voice tart.

My father paused. "I'm thinking on it," he said, his hand to his chin again. "Marius, times are not what they seem."

I let out a frustrated sigh. Were his words meant to comfort me? They left me cold. I sank into my own thoughts. Many times that first year after my mother died, I sat on the wooden bench in front of my father's fire to heat my body. I watched my father, wanting more from him, but he was quiet and dark as the shop in which he hammered, holding the thing he was working on up to the firelight, as if looking for answers.

Day by day, he hammered at his anvil, forging metal. He dipped red-hot shapes into water, pounded them into various objects, both ornate and useful: candelabra, bowls, goblets, hinges, armor, chains. . . . On occasion, he sent me to the monastery to deliver his wares. Most of the time my father was bent over his work, hunched like a tree beneath an unceasing great wind.

The fire spit a small ember to the edge of the forge.

It glowed brightly for a moment, then darkened. Papa didn't understand, didn't realize how chained I felt, didn't see how I'd grown in the past few years. Since late summer, I had nearly reached his height. My shoulders, though about as muscular as a scarecrow's, were beginning to widen.

My father's voice broke the silence. "Marius. Go find your brother."

My anger burned. I turned, pushed open the door, and let it slam behind me, leaving the warmth of the smithy behind for the cool December air.

Maybe Jean-Pierre was a little boy.

I was not.

MADAME TROUBÈNE

"**M**arius!" called Monsieur Dubois from his butcher's shop, directly across from the smithy. "Marius Poyet!" Reluctantly, I glanced in his direction. Plucked chickens, wild boar, and sausages hung from his shop rack, food mostly for wealthier merchants and noblemen.

"Why so long-faced? That brother showing signs, is he?" He laughed deeply, crazily, until he started coughing from his pig-sized belly, covered with a bloodstained apron. Others whispered about my brother, but Monsieur Dubois always teased—the way boys poke sticks at snakes, scorpions, spiders—just to see what might happen.

"Devil got your tongue?" Monsieur Dubois called. "Or did he snatch your brother from under your nose?"

I kept my distance and kept my words to myself. If I stopped too long, I'd be fed an earful of Monsieur Dubois's expert advice on ways to keep away the *loup garou*.

During the summer and fall, harvesting kept everyone occupied, but every winter, villagers turned indoors, and the warmth of their fires stirred up fearful stories. They talked about Christmas Eve, which followed on the heels of the winter solstice, the darkest day, when witches and werewolves gathered deep in the forest to celebrate with the devil himself. Villagers feared, especially on that day, that the *loup garou*, a human transformed into a blood-thirsty wolf, might enter the village or snatch a traveler from his path and rip open his throat. As Christmas Eve approached, I too had learned to watch my brother more closely.

Only a day earlier at the well, Martin, the tailor's son, had said about Jean-Pierre, "Did you see his eyes? More wolf than human." And it was true. Jean-Pierre's eyes were an unusual amber color. When the light hit them just right, they nearly glowed.

And the week before, as we sat on thatched chairs beneath the carved pulpit, Father Arnaud had said, "We must watch carefully for the devil's handiwork." Candelabra glowed with the finest beeswax candles. A tiny man, Father Arnaud's silver eyebrows, hair, and beard framed his pink, nearly translucent skin. He cast a long look at Jean-Pierre. "These are dangerous times," he said. "Through uncon-fessed sin, villagers suffer plagues and fall prey to maraud-ing soldiers. They bring it upon themselves. May God protect us!"

But on this day, I wanted to think about only myself. I wanted to feel my own wishes and dreams, not to shoulder the concerns and fears of everyone else. I ignored Mon-sieur Dubois and turned to the stairs leading up to our

home. Ivy, green even in winter, framed the arched entrance. Slowly, I climbed the stone steps, my thoughts
heavy as storm clouds. I pushed open the door.

Our chickens, one rust-headed and one black, fluttered
from atop the wooden chest at the end of Madame
Troubène's bed. Madame Troubène herself was slumped in
the chair. Her basket of yarn lay at her feet. Her spindle
sat idle. In greeting, she lifted her gray eyes from beneath
her square white headcloth, but otherwise she held her
body still before the hearth's smouldering fire.

"Marius!" cried my brother, who came running from
the hearth. His brown hair was cut square on his forehead,
his eyes as big as a deer's. "I was looking at Turkish rugs,"
he said, "and a little dog, all skinny, pushed his nose in
my hand. He needed a friend. When I looked up you were
gone. He was black with brown around his neck and—"
Words spilled from his small round mouth faster than
beans from a cloth sack.

"Slow down," I said.

"Marius, where did you go? Are we going to the ruins?"

"I spent half the morning looking for you. Let me be."

"Let's go," he pleaded and wrapped his arms around my
waist. "Marius, let's go! Maybe we'll see that dog again!
He could live with us if you asked Papa."

I clenched my hands at my sides. "I don't need to care
for a dog, too. And we don't need to feed another mouth."

"What do you have?" he asked, eyeing my hands.

"Nothing."

He pried one empty hand open, then the other, and
shrugged. "Where did you go?"

"*You* wandered off," I said.

"Was there a juggler or dance troupe? What did you see? There must have been something special, just tell me."

Straight and stiff, I fixed my gaze beyond him, refused to meet my brother's eyes. I refused to be his *mother*. Not today. Not ever again. I pushed Jean-Pierre away, roughly enough to let him know I'd grown tired of such childishness.

Jean-Pierre lost his balance and slid along the floor, piling up golden rushes and almost knocking over Madame Troubène's basket. He struggled to his knees and stood, his lower lip quivering.

I didn't want to see him cry. "Oh," I huffed. "Come here."

Jean-Pierre stepped closer. I grabbed his shoulder, spun him away from me, then lifted him under his arms. In wide circles, I swung him round and round until he began to laugh. I smiled, until the tips of his wool socks brushed Madame Troubène's long skirts.

"Has the devil begun to work in both of you?" She crossed herself. "And the moon is not yet full."

"Don't worry," I said. "We're only boys."

"Outside with you," she scolded, her voice raspy, her wooden knitting needles silent in her lap. Usually the room was filled with the click-clicking of her knitting, never missing a beat.

And where was the smell of onions and beans, *potage*, or *ragoût*? The black cauldron sat beside the fire; no steamy good smells drifted to my nose to make my mouth water. The board we ate on was stored upright beside Madame Troubène's bed. It wasn't set up on the two barrels, as usual, with three colorful tablecloths, ready for our midday meal.

Jean-Pierre curled his arms around her neck. "We're your favorite boys. That's what you always say."

"You make my head hurt," said Madame Troubène with a weak wave of her hand.

She was like a grandmother to us, but even grandmothers could turn sour as old milk.

"Don't come back with that child until the sun sets. I'm cold and I haven't—" She coughed and her headcloth shook around her ashen face. "I haven't the strength for you today."

"You should rest," I offered.

She nodded and closed her eyes.

I walked around the bench to the hearth, knelt before the dying fire, and stirred at the embers with a poker. I blew on the coals until they pulsed red, then added three logs. "There," I said. "You'll warm up soon."

From beside the door, I grabbed the leather case that held my lute and eased it over my shoulder. "We'll return in time for dinner," I said, hoping this reminder might inspire her to cook for us. Then I headed down the narrow, damp stairs with Jean-Pierre close at my heels.

Once outside, I dashed through the street.

"Wait!" Jean-Pierre called after me.

"Catch me!" I said, and in our usual game, ran. I stayed ahead, waited for a little brown head to bob around the corner, then darted off again.

THE RUINS

A week passed, and with each day that drew closer to Christmas Eve, I kept a more watchful eye on my brother.

That afternoon, in the sunny village square, I paused as a merchant lifted blankets from cages, revealing peacocks, swans, and herons, undoubtedly en route to the chateau's kitchens.

"Marius!" called Jean-Pierre. "Marius, wait!"

Again I ran, keeping ahead and glancing behind. I passed the fountain, well, and stone scaffold. To my relief, the three ropes were empty of bodies. Whenever I saw a dead body, my stomach tightened and my teeth ached. Many villagers, I knew, could walk by and not seem bothered. Not me. Death lurked always just around the corner, waiting to steal a life.

I slowed, giving Jean-Pierre a chance to get closer. From Seigneur Beaumont's house, its entrance door the tallest and widest in all the village, harpsichord music floated down. Pigeons fluttered up as I passed the house's cobblestone courtyard.

Just beyond, with the music still in my head, I nearly tripped over three dogs snarling over a bone. The smallest dog, black with brown ruff around its neck, gave up and slumped away.

I glanced back.

Jean-Pierre appeared around the street corner. "Marius!" He pointed to the dog, who crept low, then dashed off. "That's him, the one I was telling you about!"

I ignored my brother's comments and motioned to the corner of rue de Blanche, where a small crowd gathered around Jacques, the dwarf minstrel with the high voice. Jean-Pierre followed me. As the villagers quieted, I stepped close enough to listen. Jacques, nearly swallowed by his large floppy hat, blew on his wooden recorder, bringing silence, then began.

"Once," Jacques began, "there was a Roman servant, named Niceros, who loved a young woman named Melissa. One evening, Niceros decided to visit Melissa, who was staying in the country with a friend. But it was a walk of several miles, and Niceros did not want to make the journey alone, especially at night, so he persuaded his friend, a stout fellow, to join him."

Jean-Pierre brushed against my thigh and leaned into me. I didn't pull away. Jacques told the best tales.

"The moon shone bright as day and Niceros's friend star-gazed as they walked, until he fell behind. Suddenly—" Jacques paused, eyes widening, then spoke in hushed tones. The crowd didn't stir. "Niceros turned and saw his friend's clothes lying along the path, and then spotted his friend—naked—running into the woods. As his friend ran, Niceros saw him turn into a wolf and soon heard the wolf begin to howl."

A gasp rushed through the crowd.

"Niceros drew his sword"—Jacques brandished an imaginary sword—"and armed for danger, traveled bravely on to where Melissa was staying. By the time Niceros arrived at the door, sweat streamed off his body. He struggled to catch his breath.

"Melissa, his beloved, said, 'You should have come sooner. A wolf attacked the farm and has destroyed the cattle. A servant hit the wolf in the neck with a pitchfork, yet the wolf escaped.'

"As soon as Niceros heard this, he ran home. He passed the place where his friend's clothes had been, but found nothing more than a puddle of blood. Then, when Niceros got home, he found his friend lying in bed, with the doctor dressing a large wound in his friend's neck. After that, Niceros kept his distance from his friend, who he knew was a *loup garou*."

Before the villagers began to ask Jacques questions about the story, I slipped away quickly, knowing my brother would follow.

I ran out the open archway of the eastern gate, beyond the thick stone walls that had enclosed Venyre for hundreds of years. Shining on the bare olive groves and fields of grape vines, the sun rested low in the sky; we'd be back, I determined, before it set.

Within moments, Jean-Pierre neared, face flushed, breathing hard. He held his side.

18

I patted his head. "You're fast," I said, "for a snail."

Jean-Pierre tilted his head up at me. "I'm *much* faster than a snail."

"That's true. You're a lightning-fast snail."

"I hurt here," he whined, pressing his hand against his side, "as if something has its teeth in me."

"It's only a side ache," I said. "You'll be all right."

Sometimes he said the strangest things, things that made me wonder if he was truly cursed, like the man in Jacques' story.

"Someone shouted at me, Marius," he said seriously. "Did you hear?"

"No, what did they say?"

"A man held up a cross and shouted, 'Get away, you devil!'" Jean-Pierre scrunched up his face. "Why do people—"

"I don't know," I lied. "He was probably just crazy."

Jean-Pierre didn't know the truth about his real birthday, though he had begun to ask me why villagers treated him differently. Madame Troubène had started off telling him he was born on Christmas Day, not Christmas Eve, and my father had never said otherwise. But the truth couldn't be held back from him forever.

The dirt road led left toward Avignon and right toward Aix. I crossed the road, waved back to Celestin, keeper of the eastern gate, shadowed in the lookout tower above the wall's crest. He was a bulky man with a knot in his back. When he had first asked where we were going, I'd replied, "to see our mother's grave," and so Celestin had always let us come and go. The part about visiting the grave was true, but I had also come to love visiting the ruins. It was the only place we could escape the watchful eyes of the villagers.

Jean-Pierre began to skip ahead.

Washed in white light, the path wound up the eastern hill. On the crest, a round lookout tower topped the fortress, built many years ago by the Romans.

We climbed and left the barking of village dogs behind. The trail switched back, cutting between juniper and sagebrush, bare trees and bushes, some with dried red berries. I glanced back at the village; tile rooftops glinted above the walls.

Ahead, along the roadside, lay the cemetery. Gravestones, wooden crosses, and statues surrounded the tiny stone chapel. My mother rested beneath a simple cross, buried with the blessings of the Church. Wordless, we paused, heads bowed, and made the sign of the cross. Then we continued upward.

Up and up we climbed. Below us, the village shrank smaller and smaller. Breathing hard, we reached the plateau and ambled around the fortress, its walls standing square in some places, crumbling in others.

Magpies lifted in a whir of black and white feathers from the top branches of a pine tree and flew off toward the sun.

Something about the day was different than usual. The December light, perhaps, cast longer shadows. Twice, I glanced over my shoulder, thinking someone was following. I thought it was Jean-Pierre, but both times, when I turned, only bare trees stood, darkly silhouetted and twisted from wind.

Plink. Ka-chink. Jean-Pierre stood on the edge of a massive wall, and began to walk, placing one foot in front of the other, arms outstretched. Then he planted his feet and began to throw stones into the thicket below. "Marius, watch me! I'm an acrobat!"

"Get down from the ledge and be careful."

Jean-Pierre hung his head, then climbed down. He picked up another stone.

"Watch how far I can throw!"

I adjusted the lute on my back, eager for time alone.

"Marius, you're not watching," he said, reaching to the ground. He pulled back his arm as if he were going to throw a javelin, then flung another stone. *Plink.*

"Yes," I said, turning away, "you can throw."

"But you didn't even look!"

"I have other things to do, Jean-Pierre. Other things to think about." And with those words, I left him.

I climbed up sandstone rock to the tower, placed my hands on the ledge of a square stone window, and looked out. The village lay below, and for that moment, I was the ruler. I was king and seigneur. Bishop and abbot. From so high, I could see the villagers' fields; a flock of sheep on a distant slope; and the chateau to the west between towering cedar and pine, hills, and streams. To the northwest, closer yet to the ruins, sat St. Benedict's monastery; a vast expanse of fields surrounded its enclosure of buildings, where a church loomed, a cross topping its golden spire. To the northeast, the Alps glinted hazily in the distance.

I lowered the leather case from my back, untied the straps, and removed the lute. I sat down on a stone block, rested the pear-shaped lute on my lap, and ran my hand over the smooth pearly inlay of a single rose.

Holding its wooden neck, I began to pluck the strings. *Birdsong.* That's what my mother had called the lute's music. Once, when I was very small, I had gone with my father to the chateau; as he repaired a cannon, I sat entranced before a huge outdoor cage of exotic birds, colored intense shades of red, purple, yellow, and blue. I smiled to discover that the sweetest music was not coming from the most colorful birds; rather, the clearest notes came from a handful of small brown birds in the cage's corner.

I strummed the strings of my lute until music filled the stone tower, echoing, trembling, note bouncing freely against note.

Suddenly, on the breeze came a sharp scream—helpless and panicky.

Jean-Pierre.

Jumping up with my lute, I scrambled from the tower, slipped down eroded steps, and slammed my shin against a stone block.

"Jean-Pierre?" I called.

I looked across the plateau. Wild boar? A thief, or worse? Papa had warned us to always keep a careful watch, that groups of thieves and murderers wandered from village to village, stealing when they could. Dread filled me. A breeze iced along the edges of my neck. Twisted scrub oaks cast eerie shadows on the hilltop.

"Jean-Pierre!" I called again, rushed to the edge of the wall, and glanced below to the place where he'd been tossing stones. My breath caught.

On the slope, facedown beneath freshly broken branches, lay my little brother, Jean-Pierre.

Still as death.

WOLVES

"Jean-Pierre!" I shouted.

I stared at my brother, beyond my reach at the base of the wall. If only I had a rope, someone's help. The sun was beginning to sink behind reddish clouds, throwing dark shadows over the patchwork fields below. I had to hurry.

"Wait!" I called to my brother, who hadn't moved or made a sound. "I'll find some way to get to you."

I fled the wall's edge and ran across the shadowy plateau. If I could not climb down to him, I would start from below and find my way back up.

Heart pounding, I followed the dusty path that wound down, down toward the road that we'd walked together. With each stride, my lute bumped sharply against my shoulder blade.

At the cemetery, the smell of freshly turned dirt sent a chill through me. This was, I realized, the first time I had

CURSE OF A WINTER MOON

ever been near the graves alone. Always there was Jean-Pierre. Breathing hard, I made the sign of the cross and raced on.

At the south side of the ruins, I paused. My shirt clung to the sweat on my back. I looked up and studied my approach. A brown speckled hawk glided overhead. It circled over the decaying fortress and landed on the top of a leafless tree below the wall. I rubbed my palms down the sides of my face.

I could see nothing of my brother. "Always, always," I said aloud, "I'm responsible for him. If things go wrong, I'll be the one to blame." My brother's accident would be placed squarely on my shoulders.

Slowly, I made my way up, keeping an eye on the spot from where my brother had fallen. Loose rock and sand slid from beneath my leather shoes. I called as I climbed. No answer. Higher and higher I climbed, calves straining. At times I pulled myself forward on my hands and knees, glad there had been a winter freeze to keep snakes and scorpions below ground.

Scrub oaks gave way to thorny bushes. I paused and ran my hand across the front of my tan jerkin, which my father had given me when I turned twelve, the day of the grape harvest festival. I didn't want the thorns to tear the soft leather. I set down the lute, undid my rope belt and empty money purse, and pulled off my jerkin. After I found Jean-Pierre, I would come back.

I found a heavy stick and whacked at branches to clear a path. Thorns stung through my shirt. If I were an armored knight, a true chevalier, I would charge through. No pain would be too great. I envisioned myself clad in iron and pushed ahead to the base of the fortress wall.

In the distance, piercing the emptiness, a wolf's cry carried on the wind. Fear traveled up my spine. Maybe it was calling to my brother. Trembling, I touched my own neck. How I wished I were wearing a cross, or a wolf's tooth.

I hurried.

In the last shades of light, I came upon Jean-Pierre. He lay chest down with his head turned sideways. Blood painted the edge of his mouth. His playful voice and smile were gone. He didn't move.

I froze. I had no idea what to do.

Another wolf howled. Closer. Its call—low and long— sounded like a minstrel's saddest song. It seemed to be coming from the plateau above us, but with the wind, I couldn't be sure. My heart pulsed faster.

Slowly, I inched backward, not taking my eyes from my brother. My mind flooded with a memory of the time a man had fallen into the church aisle. *That* man. Back arched, eyes rolled white, with blood coming from his mouth, as if he had bitten his tongue. In the hush, Brother Gabriel, my uncle from St. Benedict's, had stepped seemingly out of nowhere toward the man. His cross hung squarely over his vestment, protecting him. He had quietly asked for the help of two men, who carried the man's rigid body away. The mass had continued, but after the man had been removed, the candles had seemed to glow more brightly. Whispers of *"loup garou"* hovered in the sanctuary. Maybe the devil was working in my brother in the same way. Maybe the wolves were calling to him. I couldn't be too careful.

There had to be something—a prayer, a magic spell, a holy relic—something that would help. Only last summer, I'd studied a special ring at the market, engraved with words I could not read; its one-eyed owner claimed it would keep werewolves away. If only I'd had enough money.

More than anything, I wanted to run back to the village, to safety. I began to walk away, quietly, slowly at first, but with increasing speed. Then it struck me. Brother Gabriel had acted calm in the face of danger, in the face of evil itself. He hadn't fled. I stopped.

In the distance, the sun was gone, leaving only a pool of deep purple and red behind. If I didn't return with my brother, and if villagers also heard the wolves, before morning the hillside might be swarming with villagers carrying scythes and swords in search of the *loup garou*. I looked toward the village where the gate torches now glowed.

I walked cautiously back to where Jean-Pierre lay as limp as a rag. I held my breath.

Somewhere far off, wolves howled again. A single wolf's cry sliced the air and it was quickly joined by another, then another, until it sounded as if a thousand wolves were in the distant hills, calling to Jean-Pierre to join them. My mind crept to two questions I could never answer: What if the villagers were right about him? And, if my brother turned, would I defend myself . . . kill the *loup garou*?

"Marius?" came a frightened voice. "Marius?" repeated Jean-Pierre, rising on his elbows, then falling back.

"Here I am," I said, relieved to hear his voice. Still, I kept myself behind the rock, just to be safe.

"I don't"—Jean-Pierre's voice was weak—"feel well." He touched his forehead, then slumped lifeless to the ground.

My throat tightened with tears. Here was my brother, my only brother, and he needed my help. Suddenly, I didn't care about the risks.

I leaped out from behind the rock, scooped up Jean-Pierre, and shouldered his body down the slope toward the glow of the village below.

CAGED MEN

December 22

I woke to a bite behind my left ear, sat upright, yanked a small black tick from my skin, and flung it to the far side of the room. At the foot of Madame Troubène's bed, the redheaded chicken stretched its wings slightly and flapped to the floor. Head bobbing, it pecked among the rushes.

Beside me slept Jean-Pierre, mouth wide open. Since I had carried him back from the ruins two days earlier, like Madame Troubène he had mostly slept, asking only for a drink of broth now and then. Gratefully, I had escaped questioning. My father had taken to rising early and returning late.

I leaned over and began searching my brother's scalp for lice. As I did, I studied his face again. His right eye was swollen shut and purplish blue with a tint of green; his gashed forehead had scabbed over. That first night back, blood had dried in a mess across his dirt-streaked face. I had cleaned off the dried blood, but he still looked terrible.

In my mind, I could still hear the cries of the wolves. I tried to brush the memory away, not to dwell on the night at the ruins or on my own fears. As it was, the past two nights I'd barely slept, waking every few moments to look over at Jean-Pierre, to lift the blanket and see if he was changing into a wolf, or into something half human, half beast.

Jean-Pierre stirred, breathed in noisily through his nose, and opened his right eye. He touched his forehead. "My head hurts, Marius. Wh-what happened?"

I exhaled with a smile. Finally, he was speaking. I never thought I would miss his voice.

"Don't you remember?" I tried to keep my voice low so as not to wake Madame Troubène. "You fell and . . . and . . . I carried you home."

"I remember throwing stones," he whispered, closing his good eye. "That's all."

I frowned. My brother looked tired. How could he remember nothing at all? My heart tightened. I hoped his sudden failing in memory was not part of some deep magic. "Go back to sleep," I said.

With that, Jean-Pierre disappeared beneath the blanket. Soon, his chest began to rise and fall slowly, rhythmically. I lay down, pulled the blanket over my shoulder, and began to drift to sleep.

Hours later, shouts rose from the streets. I jumped up, careful not to wake Jean-Pierre, and hurried past Madame Troubène's bed. After my mother's death, my father insisted that Madame Troubène use their wood-frame bed; he slept on the smaller mattress, which was now empty.

He must have left again before dawn.

I unbolted the shutters. My breath formed a misty cloud of white as I looked out. Villagers were pouring into the street, crowding around a caravan of travelers. My first thought was that they were traveling minstrels, but I caught sight of the figure of a monk robed completely in black, atop a black horse with a white star. The sun fell upon the monk's wide forehead, revealing a red birthmark, somewhat like the imprint of a baby's hand. This man wasn't a simple monk. He had to be the abbot.

A chevalier followed, his armor glinting silver-white. His horse pranced left and sideways down the street, ten paces, then the knight reined the horse, and the animal pranced right, another ten paces. Next walked a trumpeter with a flag of bright red and yellow hanging from his horn. *Bum-bum-bum-breeee! Bum-bum-bum-breee!* A cart and driver, four armed men on horseback, and a handful of soldiers walking alongside made up the rest of the procession.

Too curious to stay inside, I closed the shutters, threw on my breeches and shoes, and raced down the stairs to get a closer look.

The smell of refuse pinched my nose—bitingly strong—for every morning villagers poured their night pails into the streets below. In summer, the smells ripened, and when merchants, nobles, and ladies visited, they pressed pomanders filled with spices and dried flowers to their noses. Winter air was better.

Pulling a cart, a pair of large tan horses with black manes and tails muscled toward me through the dung. The horses added their steaming manure to the streets as they passed by. Behind the wagon's driver were two wooden crates on a flatbed wagon.

I stared. Each crate held a man.

Just as the wagon passed, one of the caged men looked up and met my eyes. His skin hung loosely on his nearly naked bony frame. I shivered in my shirt and breeches, but his clothing was little more than shredded rags. Lips leathery and chalky white, he slowly mouthed one word: "Water."

"He needs water," I said to anyone who would listen. Who were these men? What had they done? I'd seen criminals tied up, walking behind a procession or tied up on a wagon, but not caged.

I walked alongside the cart, which stopped near the well, and continued to watch the man. His eyes, set deep in a gaunt face, searched mine. In my mind, as clear as church bells, I heard the words Father Arnaud had recently spoken at mass: "Whatever you do for the least of them, you do for me." *Christ's words.* If this man was thirsty, then clearly it was my Christian duty to offer him drink.

I ran to the well, where Marguerite, a weaver and once a good friend of my mother's, hoisted a wooden bucket overflowing with water. She set it on the well's rim, then tucked a loose black curl into the edge of her white cap.

"May I?" I asked, cupping my hands to her.

"Of course, Marius," she said. Her smile vanished when she turned her head toward the caged men.

"Merci." I filled my hands with water from her bucket and hurried to the cart.

"Marius," came Marguerite's voice, carrying a warning.

Water dripped through my fingers, but with just a sip

left, I pushed my hands into the cart toward the man's mouth. He licked droplets from my palms.

Suddenly, a steely blow knocked me to the ground. A sharp pain flared in my shoulder. Wooden wagon wheels jolted forward through the dirt, dangerously close to my head.

Stumbling to my feet, my head and side covered with smelly dung, I met the eyes of a mercenary.

Thick-set, filling out his black jerkin, which he wore over puffy breeches and high black boots, the mercenary grabbed the gilded handle of his sword that hung from his side. "Keep away!" he barked, sinews straining in his neck.

I cowered, expecting the man to pierce me through with his sword.

"Keep away from the heretics!" he said, turning to the small circle of villagers that had formed. I lowered my eyes.

"You."

I looked up.

The mercenary pointed his sword at me. "Don't make me put you in a cage alongside them. They'll likely die before sundown, but not before we get a confession out of them," he said. "On second thought, I would be paid even better for a third heretic, wouldn't I?" Then he laughed, spat, and moved on with the procession.

A heretic was a dangerous person, someone who went against the ways of the Church, to be damned forever. There had been more talk of heretics every Sunday, but these were the first ones I'd seen. Yet the caged men didn't look as dangerous as this mercenary.

Ahead, the horn blew from the square. I ran to where the crowd was gathering.

"Let this be a warning!" came a booming voice. The procession stopped at the steps of the fountain.

"Abbot Joseph," whispered a woman beside me, who leaned on her stick and clutched at her cloak around her neck.

"I have just returned from travels," the abbot called, his arms stretched wide in his black frock before the growing audience. "Sickness has swept through a village to the south! Bodies piled outside their walls! Even now, wolves are feasting on the flesh of the dead."

He paused. The audience waited silently.

"Let this be a warning," the abbot continued. "Take care to follow God's ways, good people of Venyre. If there is evil in our midst, do not give it time to fester, especially as Christmas Eve draws near."

The woman beside me crossed herself. "Holy Mother Mary," she whispered under her breath. Others kneeled to the ground, heads bowed.

I wasn't used to hearing a sermon in the streets. The presence of the abbot, speaking to the villagers, sent a thrill of urgency through me. This was important, a time of spiritual battle, a time for villagers to unite. But with the mention of Christmas Eve, I worried about Jean-Pierre. I pushed the thoughts away and wrapped my arms tightly over my chest.

"Be on guard," Abbot Joseph continued. "We have heard of Huguenot activity right here in Venyre. Anyone suspected of being a heretic will be brought to trial. To protect you, we will rout them from among us. See these men? Let them be judged by the Holy Church and God."

Shouting and cursing rose from the streets. At the

wagon with the caged men, a peasant named Adrien, who himself wore nothing better than a hole-riddled jerkin and wool tights that bagged around his ankles, rapped on the cages with a long stick—*whack, whack*—then poked at the men. Others spat at them. Then the abbot and the procession moved forward.

I stood, transfixed. Huguenots? Weren't they nearly as dangerous as werewolves? Huguenots were the heretics I'd heard about. They didn't believe in following the Holy Church. I'd heard travelers, less careful with their speech, talking about the Huguenot leaders: John Calvin and Martin Luther. Some said they danced with the devil himself. They didn't believe in the pope, and supposedly they didn't believe that the bread and wine served at Communion were the very body and blood of Christ. Some villagers said Huguenots met in secret to drink *real* blood. I didn't know much, really, about them. But I knew they were to be feared.

I turned my palms up. A horror crept through me. I'd let the caged man's lips touch my hands. He'd licked my fingers like an animal. My mind swam. I tried to swallow, but my throat had turned dusty dry. Cursed. Perhaps I was now cursed, stamped by Satan. What a fool I'd been to give that man—if he could be called that—a drink. Maybe I'd brought curses not only on myself, but perhaps upon my whole village.

Vigorously, I rubbed my hands together, harder and harder, until flecks of dirt rolled up like black gnats and fell to the ground. I rubbed my hands until my palms and fingers turned from blackish gray to grayish pink. Finally, I stopped and looked around.

The woman beside me was gone. The whole crowd had moved on.

I met only the eyes of the small black dog—Jean-Pierre's dog—curled tightly on the stone doorstep of a house across from the fountain. He whined, but I didn't encourage him. He thumped his tail, but he didn't rise to his legs. I avoided his eyes. I didn't have any scraps to feed him anyway. I wasn't a nobleman who could pamper a dog with full meals. He whimpered, then tucked his nose into the curve of his body.

Forcing myself to turn away, I then slunk like a stray cat alongside the edges of the stone buildings and shops. I returned to the well, poured a bucket of water over my hands, then walked down the street to the narrow stairs leading home.

I stepped into silence. Madame Troubène was still sleeping, and Jean-Pierre was gone. Even the blanket we shared was gone. The small leather shoes were missing. Had he run off again? Every time I turned my back, he disappeared. I had been gone only a short time. Did he step out, or had he vanished, the curse of his birth taking hold?

With all the noise outside the window, perhaps Jean-Pierre had gone out to explore, had journeyed into the crowd. I chewed at a ragged fingernail.

The crowd. In one moment, villagers could be at church, moved to their knees and willing to endure great suffering for their sins, and in the next moment, they could rise up in anger and drag the guilty to the scaffold. Papa was right, of course, but I did not want to admit it. With so many watchful eyes on my brother, I could only fear what might happen. *Take good care of your brother.*

THE BOX

I searched the market square, the first place Jean-Pierre would wander. He loved jugglers and acrobats more than anything. With the commotion around the morning caravan, he would have followed the noise, thinking it was entertainment. But he wasn't there.

I returned past the mill and butcher's shop, head down. My task was impossible. No one could keep his eye on a six-year-old from dawn to dusk, unless, of course, he were an angel.

At my father's smithy, pounding sounded within. I eased open the door. Light filtered in through a small window and dust danced in the shaft that fell on my father's workbench. My father dipped a shield into the large wooden vat of water. *Pffft! Hisss!* Steam blasted the air.

I drew in a deep breath, even though the air was dense with smoke. For only a moment, here, in this place where the fire was warm, where my father worked steadily, I sensed that everything was good, that any problem could be eased away. Reworked. Reshaped.

Steam cleared and my eyes adjusted to the dim light. Beyond my father, curled on a blanket beside the fire, was Jean-Pierre.

"You little maggot!" I scolded. "I've searched every street of Venyre looking for you!"

Jean-Pierre turned from the fire and hopped up.

"You should have waited for me to—"

He hugged my waist. "But you always find me."

"Even so, you shouldn't run off!" I scolded. Then my voice softened. "You must wait for me. I didn't know where . . ." Emotion rose in my chest and my voice caught. I tousled my brother's hair, squatted down, and looked into his face.

Beneath bruises and swelling, his amber eyes probed mine. He gently placed his hands to the sides of my face. "Don't worry, Marius," he said. "You worry too much."

I didn't have a response. Sometimes my brother's ways, his constant cheerfulness and steadiness, amazed me. Times like this, he seemed older than his years. He hugged my neck and whispered in my ear, "Ask Papa about that dog." Then, without his usual pestering and questions, he walked back to the wool blanket stretched on the dirt floor before the fire and lay down.

"What happened?" asked my father, with a nod toward my brother.

I stepped closer, and quietly told about Jean-Pierre's fall, but left out what had scared me the most; that perhaps the wolves were calling to him. I couldn't bring myself to speak this aloud. Not even to my own father. "Truly, I think he's fine," I concluded.

"You must keep a closer eye on him."

"But . . ." I didn't want to hear any more. Didn't my father see how hard I tried to do just that? I walked to the edge of the forge in front of Jean-Pierre, who to my surprise was already sleeping, his mouth wide open, as usual. I stirred the dusty-red embers with the poker.

Jean-Pierre was right—I did worry. When it came to my brother, I always felt like I was hanging on to the horns of a bull. If I let go, what might happen? If I hung on, at least the bull couldn't run me through. I shrugged off my own strange thoughts. For all that I knew, all that I'd seen, my mind was torn. Madame Troubène was certain of his curse; sometimes he said the strangest things; villagers talked; even the priest seemed to know. Still, I sensed no evil in Jean-Pierre. Even so, I needed to be watchful.

"I need your help," said my father, cutting me off from my thoughts, an urgency in his voice. "I need you to deliver something." With blackened hands, he set aside the shield he was working on. "First," he said, "bolt the door."

I obeyed.

He stepped to a corner chest, lifted the lid, and brought out a wooden box, strapped tightly with leather strips. "Take this to St. Benedict's," he whispered, "and ask for Brother Gabriel. He will be there."

"A candleholder?" I asked. I took the box, not much heavier than a small iron pot.

"Give it only to Brother Gabriel," my father continued. "No one else. Do you understand?"

My chest filled and I stood taller. My father was

entrusting me with an important task. Perhaps he was sending me to deliver an item he'd been perfecting in the late hours. That explained his returning to bed so late, his rising extra early. Perhaps his talent had caught the attention of the abbot. "Yes, Papa."

I glanced at my sleeping brother.

Before I could ask, my father said, "Until Madame Troubène feels better, Jean-Pierre can stay here.

"Stay clear of strangers. Walk on the road only when necessary, otherwise, keep to the woods and fields."

"Yes, of course."

"Once you get there, ask Brother Gabriel about the box. You're old enough to know, and he can better explain its contents than I can."

Then my father kissed me on each side of my face, turned abruptly away, and with iron clamps, lifted the shield to the light. It was simple, perhaps belonging to the gatekeeper, and its corner was dented. He set it back on the coals.

I hesitated at the door, the box in my hands, and wondered at my father's words. I looked out, left and right, then stepped back in for a moment, the box in my hands. "Papa?" I asked. "Did you see the caged men?"

He continued working. "Yes. Yes, I saw them."

"Someone said they're Huguenots—heretics. They're evil, right Papa?"

My father looked up, his brown eyes somber with an intensity I had never seen before. "I only know one thing," he said firmly. "They're men."

Again, from the embers he lifted the shield. Its edge glowed red, as if it were alive, then quickly began to fade.

"But aren't they dangerous . . . aren't they—"

"Go," he said. "Now."

"Yes, Papa."

I stepped into the full light, my lute strapped on my back. Just for good measure, I shifted the wooden box to my left hand, then with my right made the sign of the cross. In times such as these, I needed all the protection I could get. I studied the streets for the caged men and the mercenary, who were nowhere in sight, then walked quickly toward the eastern gate, glad to finally leave my brother behind.

Still, strangely enough, something nameless nagged at me. For all the moments I had wished to be free of my responsibility, now that it was suddenly lifted, a tinge of worry seeped like rainwater into a well-worn path.

Brother Gabriel

By midmorning, when the sun had driven cold from the air, I found myself in steady stride along the road. In the surrounding fields, grape vines were pruned, waiting for spring. Olive trees stood bare after the late November harvest; their meaty pulp had been pressed between sheets and turned into Venyre's famous olive oil.

Midway over a wooden bridge, its boards rutted with wheel marks, I paused. Water rushed beneath me, gurgling, as if it had a mind of its own, racing from the mountains toward the Rhône River and the Mediterranean. My mother once said "the sea sparkles like an endless jewel." Unlike the other village women, she was born beyond Venyre, had lived near the sea, and had left behind a wealthier life to marry my father, bringing along only her lute and her nanny, Madame Troubène. Someday, perhaps my feet would carry me beyond Venyre. With the box tucked beneath my arm, I journeyed toward the monastery, lost in thought.

Ahead, the monastery steeple rose tall above the stone walls. As I neared the oak gates, I noticed the carving of a saint with a halo—St. Benedict himself, who left the city of Rome to dwell in a cave. The cave was still said to be able to heal those who visit it.

I thought again about the man at church. For weeks after Brother Gabriel had removed the man from mass, villagers spoke about "the miracle." They said God had sent an angel in the form of a visiting monk to spare the village. I knew the monk was not an angel. "That was my uncle, Brother Gabriel," I'd explained to one country peasant selling squash. "Oh, no," she'd replied, crossing herself, "mark my words, it was an angel." If villagers often jumped to such ridiculous conclusions, then surely not all of their notions could be true.

For a long time, I had wanted to ask my uncle about the man who had begun to turn into a *loup garou*, right there in the sanctuary. But I rarely saw my uncle, who traveled widely, and passed like a shadow in and out of my father's shop once or twice a year. On my errands to the monastery, he was usually away. Surely Brother Gabriel must have special prayers, a special cross, something. I did not believe Jean-Pierre could be like that man, but still, was it not my job to watch over my brother? With the right thing, I might be able to protect him.

I pulled the bell rope, which hung above the gate, and the bell rang out, clear and loud. A small panel in the door slid open, and a young monk looked out, a boy about my age, but taller, with auburn hair and a generously freckled nose. I had seen him once before. "Welcome to the Lord's house and to St. Benedict's," he said.

"Bonjour," I said. "I am to deliver this"—I lifted the wooden box to the window— "to Brother Gabriel."

"Please enter," the young monk said. He eyed the lute on my back. "A musician?"

"I play . . . some," I said.

The doors opened wide, and I stepped into the stone courtyard. Small trees and shrubs lined the inner walls. A dozen buildings filled the monastery, but the church took center stage. It towered on a foundation of massive stones; its spire rose nearly to heaven. To the left of the church ran a long row of arched columns. At the end of the row, a cluster of monks stood talking; each wore a hooded cowl and brown frock, sashed at the waist with a white rope, and a simple wooden cross.

"Wait here," the boy said, then turned and stalked away like a crane, his skinny ankles protruding like stilts beneath the brown frock he must have recently outgrown. He disappeared beyond the white arched pillars, which framed a garden filled with evergreen shrubs.

My stomach growled. I had not eaten yet that day.

The monastery was quiet. My village was glaringly noisy compared to this holy place. I wondered if I was doing anything wrong. I shifted uncomfortably from one foot to the next, then tried to stand still.

The young monk returned. "You may call me Augustin," he said.

"My name is Marius," I said, with a slight nod. "Marius Poyet."

43

"Brother Gabriel will be with you soon. Until then, I'm to keep you company."

For a brief time, we were silent.

Augustin glanced beyond the walls of the monastery to the cloud-streaked sky beyond, as if searching for words. He cleared his throat, then spoke. "I like the lute," he volunteered. "I'm told my voice, too, is an instrument." His smile stretched wide, then faltered, then fell. "Abbot Joseph wants me to sing for the Sistine choir."

"You'd sing for the pope?" I could only wish for such an opportunity. "That's wonderful!" Other boys were moving on to apprenticeships, some moving on to sing in choirs for the pope. I felt left behind.

"Well, yes, for the pope, though I would first go to Avignon," he said. "I have to decide soon, I'm told. Very soon."

I shrugged my shoulders and laughed. "To use your voice for the pope himself? What is there to decide?"

Augustin clamped his perfect front teeth over his lower lip, exhaled hard, then whispered, "I would have to choose to become a . . . a *castrat*."

My enthusiasm disappeared. A *castrat*. Some time ago my father had explained the word. A *castrat* was a boy whose maleness had been partly removed, cut off, in order to keep his high, clear voice for the Church choir. I shuddered. "Wh-what will you do?"

He wore the look of a prisoner destined to wear chains. "I'm told my singing is my greatest calling, that it would be a small sacrifice, but I'm not sure. And with the abbot . . . and his love for music"—he glanced around, as if to make sure no one was listening—"I'm not sure if it's a choice or a command."

Just then, another monk, closer to my father's age, walked toward us. Beneath the cowl, his head—like the others—was shaved. He smiled, only one tooth missing, with dimples as deep as craters, and I recognized him. My mother, I suddenly remembered, had had the same dimples. A pang pierced me. I missed her.

Brother Gabriel met my eyes. *"Bonjour,"* he said. "Your father said he would soon send you." He smiled again. "I haven't seen you in two years or better. Your straight nose, your thick dark hair—you're so much like her." He paused, touched my shoulder lightly. "And I see you're still playing the lute, Marius. Good, good." He tilted his head wistfully and smiled. "It's been in our family a long, long time." Then he pulled himself from his thoughts and stood straight. He eyed the box, still in my hands. "Come, we'll talk in my study."

I walked silently beside my uncle.

"I see you met Augustin," he said.

"He's so young—my age."

"He was given to the monastery when he was quite small. His mother dedicated him to God."

"He's a monk, then?"

"Not quite," said Brother Gabriel. "But soon. When he is old enough to take his vows."

Down one corridor, then another, I followed. I passed rooms with long benches, fireplaces, and tapestry-covered walls. In some hallways, monks sat at study tables, writing or reading. One older monk snored over an open scroll. I passed statues of the Virgin Mary, Joseph, Jesus, and saints I couldn't name. I tried to take it all in, the grandness, the awesomeness of this place.

Brother Gabriel pushed open a wooden door to a small room. As many as fifteen books were securely chained on a shelf. Two were stacked on a table. A real table. Not a board laid on supports, but a table with carved legs.

Light filtered through a stained-glass window and shone blue on a quill and a parchment held wide with stones, one on each corner. Writing that I couldn't read was on the parchment, drying.

"You're a teacher?" I asked, remembering what my father had said of my uncle.

"Of sorts." Brother Gabriel smiled. "A scholar. I travel from monastery to monastery, sometimes to Rome. I teach other monks and counsel with abbots and bishops. Mostly, I study the Holy Scriptures . . ." He shut the door quietly behind him and sat at the desk. " . . . As well as the works of learned thinkers." He pointed to a small chest. "Sit, please," he said. "Tell me about yourself."

I cleared my throat and sat down. It wasn't the custom for an adult to speak so much with a younger person. What would I say? That I was my younger brother's keeper, maid, and mother? That I desperately wanted to become an apprentice, to begin the journey to manhood? It would all sound foolish. I opened my mouth, but nothing came out.

Brother Gabriel laughed warmly and his dimples deepened. "Pardon me. I've made you uncomfortable." He sat in the chair. "Perhaps I've spent too many years behind monastery walls."

I extended the small box to him. "My father wanted . . ."

He took it in his hands and rested it in the lap of his frock. Bluish veins etched his pale hands like marble. "Do you know the contents of the box?"

"No," I said. My mind turned to another subject. My brother.

"Ah, I would like to show you, but" —Brother Gabriel held up his forefinger— "it could be risky. Some would not approve. Are you old enough to discuss such things? Your father must think so, or I doubt he would have sent you."

"You can trust me," I blurted. "He told me to ask you about it, that I'm old enough."

Brother Gabriel nodded, then undid the leather straps tied fast around the box. He rested his hands on the lid and seemed to study me. I met his gaze and waited. Finally, he opened the box.

I watched. Nothing sparkled or gleamed. As the lid came off, I noted three books, leather-bound, inside. Books, I knew, were a rare possession. I certainly had never held one myself, but why would my father, a blacksmith, pass along this kind of thing to Brother Gabriel? As far as I knew, my father had no use for books, even though he possessed a keener mind than most villagers.

"Two books and a Bible," said Brother Gabriel. "Written in French, printed on a press." He opened the pages and I saw neat, small, clear letters in straight thin lines. "For you or your father or anyone in the village to have books would be suspect, but to have a Bible would be heresy."

I nodded. "Yes, of course."

"For some members of the clergy, it's a threat to their

power, especially if the Bible is read in a language other than Latin, something the people can understand," Brother Gabriel said. "The Holy Church forbids interpreting the Word on one's own. Guidance must come only through the Church. To others, reading the Bible is enlightenment."

"But why did my father . . ." I faltered. My heart beat harder.

"Marius, he borrowed them from me," Brother Gabriel said gently. "He finished reading them. Most likely he sent them with you—at some risk, I might add—so they wouldn't be found."

My eyes widened. "Reading them?" My head swam with new knowledge. I rubbed my hands together, palms sweaty. "Hardly anyone in the village can read," I said, more to myself than to my uncle. "Only the monks and priests, the nobility, sometimes a traveler. I don't believe . . . not my own father."

"Your mother and I were born to a noble family," said Brother Gabriel. "When Isabelle chose to marry your father, who worked then at our chateau, she was forced to leave her wealth and her family behind. But she took with her something of greater value. She could read. She taught your father to read and intended to teach you, as well, and would have, had she not died so young."

I was stunned. Silence hovered in the air. "My mother could read?" I said. "Lived at a chateau?" I rose to my feet and began pacing. I knew she had come from a family of greater means. But nobility? And she had taught my father to read?

Suddenly I stopped and met the monk's eyes. "If my

father can read, if he can read Scripture, doesn't that make
my father . . ." I couldn't speak the word, not out loud.

"A heretic?" offered the monk. "To some," he said and
shook his head with a sad smile. "Certainly not to me."

Suddenly, I felt nearly dizzy with thoughts. Heretics,
Huguenots, the *loup garou.* "My father," I said, "must not
have wanted the books, the Bible, to be found, that's why
he wanted them gone."

Brother Gabriel studied me.

"But why would he break the rules, why would he put
his life—and mine—in danger, just to read?"

"For love . . . for freedom," my uncle said slowly, "a
man will risk everything." He paused. "Your father does
not want to endanger you. He waited as long as possible
to reveal these things."

I closed my eyes, steadied myself. A numbing iciness
rose up from the floor through my whole being. My vision
became watery. Heavily, I sat down on the chest and
buried my face in my hands.

THE ABBOT

Moments passed. Footsteps passed outside the door of Brother Gabriel's study. Before long, I lifted my head.

"For now, enough talk of these things," said Brother Gabriel, fingering the silver cross that hung over his chest. "The Benedictine way is to offer any guest a night's lodging and a good meal. Of course you'll want to return home soon, but are you hungry?"

I still needed to discuss Jean-Pierre with my uncle, but my stomach growled loudly in protest.

"There's your answer," my uncle said, holding the door ajar. "Here, let me take you to the kitchen."

Before long, I was sitting on a bench at a long table. A monk placed a banquet before me on a wooden trencher: two chicken legs, a piece of herring, and two eggs. Beside this was a large bowl of sausage *potage* and a loaf of bread made from finely ground wheat flour.

"Is this food all for me?" I asked. It was more than I could have imagined.

"Of course." My uncle smiled.

I dove in with both hands, ate the *potage* with a wooden spoon, finished everything except half the loaf of bread, then washed it all down with a mug of cider.

"Enough?" said Brother Gabriel, seated across from me.

I patted my belly. "More than enough." I eyed the half loaf that remained.

"Take it for your walk home," my uncle offered.

I tucked it into the square pocket of my jerkin. I'd never eaten bread so fine; our usual fare was coarse and gritty, as if the grain had been swept off the floor. "*Merci!*"

Before I left, I needed to ask a greater question, though I feared the answer. "Brother Gabriel," I began, "can . . . can a person born on Christmas Eve . . . can he not escape becoming a *loup garou?*"

"Your brother?" asked Brother Gabriel asked gravely.

At first I didn't answer. A monk waited at the edge of the kitchen. Could I talk freely here about Jean-Pierre? I looked at my uncle, his eyes trustworthy.

"Yes," I finally said, and sat still, hands folded at the edge of the table, as if in prayer. Despite being full, my stomach tightened. "That man that you helped at church, the one villagers said was turning into . . ."

"Oh yes, I tried."

"What happened to him?" I pressed. "Did he change shape once he was removed from mass? Did you say a prayer, use holy water, or a blessed cross?"

Brother Gabriel puckered his chin and shook his head.

"Nothing quite that dramatic," he said. "He was ill, and seizures came upon him from time to time. It was best to keep him calm and let it pass."

"Was he born on Christmas Eve, like Jean-Pierre?"

My uncle shook his head.

"Had he drunk from a wolf print when it filled with rainwater?"

Again, my uncle shook his head. "No, I don't believe so," he said calmly, steadily, as if these things didn't cause him to tremble at all.

"We brought him here to our infirmary. He was fully human, but having violent seizures. We tried to help him, poor man, but nonetheless he died. Died as all of us will do someday. And so we hang on to eternal hope, as we do for your mother, for the life beyond this one."

The image of my mother—her braid falling over her shoulder as she strummed the lute, just for me—filled my mind. For a moment, my own fears suddenly melted away, then my mind returned to what Brother Gabriel had said.

The man at church hadn't turned into a *loup garou*. He was *sick*, not cursed as so many villagers, including Madame Troubène, had insisted. Brother Gabriel's ideas startled me, yet they made sense.

Brother Gabriel rose heavily and turned to one of the dining room windows. He rested his hands on the stone ledge. "Christ came to bring light in the darkness," he said. "And that light continues spreading. The light shines through France's own John Calvin—"

I couldn't believe he'd said it. *John Calvin.* A name one shouldn't speak aloud.

"—And Jacques Lefèvre d'Etaples, who died years ago," my uncle continued, "but who translated the Bible into French for everyone to read."

Brother Gabriel turned, tucking both hands into his frock's shadowy sleeves. I shivered, aware suddenly of the draftiness in the monastery.

"The light, dear Marius, shines brighter every day . . . except, I fear, in some places, in some small corners, such as Venyre, where it is still quite dark. Since your brother was born on Christmas Eve, you have more to fear, it would seem, from the villagers themselves than from your brother."

Outside the stained-glass window, a mourning dove cooed.

"I'm afraid," he said, "you must be on guard, Marius, not only for your brother, but for yourself as well." He removed his hands from his sleeves and pressed his palms together, fingers spread wide. "With just the right wind, Marius, fear spreads like grass fire."

Then he nodded at the monk waiting at the edge of the kitchen, who cleared away my mug. I glanced back; the meal had tasted so good.

"Come," said Brother Gabriel, and he led me toward the entrance gates.

Brother Augustin flashed me a smile and fidgeted with the cloth of his frock, as if he wanted to talk. But he looked up at Brother Gabriel and unbolted the wooden doors instead. My uncle kissed me on each cheek. "Greet your father for me . . . and little Jean-Pierre."

"I will."

Standing in the open gate, I adjusted the lute on my back. Hoofbeats drummed the ground. I turned.

At a full gallop, dust piling up like storm clouds behind it, a black horse with a white star nearly charged into me. I flattened myself against one of the wooden doors, beside Brother Gabriel.

The rider wore a frock, its hood pulled back from his round face. Three rabbits hung down the horse's side. I recognized the horse and rider from the morning procession.

"Abbot Joseph," whispered Brother Gabriel.

Over the abbot's shoulder was a bow and a quiver of arrows. A lanky monk hurried to the horse and held its reins as the abbot swung down, and then the monk led the lathered horse away.

The abbot headed through the courtyard and called out, "I'm hungry as a bear!"

Rising from a bench in the courtyard, a woman approached in a hooped blue gown, the skirt padded full at her hips; from below her waist, a V-shaped bodice rose to a low, square neckline. On her white bosom rested a string of shimmery red jewels. She snuggled beneath the chin of the abbot. He drew her close to his side, his hand nearly engulfing her waist, and kissed her neck, then walked with her through the stone courtyard, the woman's laughter sharp as broken pottery.

I stared after them, knowing I'd just seen more than my own lips should ever speak.

Just then, the abbot stopped and turned. "You there!" he called, looking back at me, Brother Gabriel, and Augustin.

My uncle silently took a step forward, then waited.

"No, the village boy," the abbot said.

I froze. What had I done? Fear flashed through me. Would I be flogged for watching?

"Do you play that instrument, or just tote it on your back?" called the abbot.

I swallowed and cleared my dry throat. "I play . . . some," I called, my voice weaker than I'd intended.

"Are you any good?"

I didn't answer. I had never played for a real audience. What was I to say?

The abbot waved away my silence. "Don't bother to answer. I'll be the judge of that. Come! Play for me while I dine."

Monastery bells began to chime. The abbot turned and strode away with the woman.

I gave my uncle a questioning look. "I need to return," I said. The thought of playing for the abbot unleashed a swarm of bees in my stomach. My heart pulsed in my ears. "My brother wasn't well," I said, "and my father will worry if . . ."

"Don't cross Abbot Joseph," my uncle said, placing his hand on my shoulder. "You must go. And I must go to prayer."

He gently gripped my elbow and steered me away from the gate and back into the monastery's interior.

Behind us, I heard Augustin shut and bolt the entrance doors.

"Just remember," my uncle said with an apologetic look. "Not everything here is the Benedictine way. Remember that."

THE LUTE

I quickened my steps past the sanctuary door, where Brother Gabriel slipped behind a stream of monks of all shapes, ages, and sizes. Suddenly, I was alone. From within the church, voices rose in Latin chanting, a song that was both sad and comforting. I wanted to linger, to listen.

Instead, I hurried after the bright blue of the woman's dress as she walked arm in arm with the abbot.

They turned into a doorway and the woman laughed, but nothing in her laughter seemed warm or inviting. Perhaps she was with the abbot out of love, but this reason seemed unlikely. I had heard talk of such things. Perhaps she wasn't there on her own free will. Perhaps she was part of a bargain, offering herself to the abbot to keep someone she loved from prison.

I slowed my step, stopped outside the open door, and cleared my throat.

"Good of you to join us!" exclaimed the abbot. "Come in." The room held a massive table.

I stood beside an embroidered tapestry that glinted with threads of gold. I tried not to breathe. Slowly, I wiped my damp palms on the sides of my breeches, aware that I lacked the colorful clothing of a respected musician, and prayed my fingers would not slip on the strings.

I tried not to think about what the villagers whispered. They said that Abbot Joseph wouldn't allow peasants to glean from the monastery fields after harvest. He fined harshly, and tripled the tithe on Church holidays (of which we celebrated nearly a hundred each year). He often oversaw the torture chamber in the belly of the monastery, as well as in the village guardhouse. The abbot also required widows, upon the death of their husbands, to donate the husband's bed to the monastery. Clearly, Abbot Joseph had little regard for clerical rules against hunting animals or having female companions.

Within moments, a half-dozen monks arrived and set platters of food upon the table: roasted pheasant, meat pie, orange marmalade, golden loaves of bread, a blue-and-white earthenware bottle.

The abbot poured red wine from the bottle into his goblet. He drank, offered the goblet to the woman, then circled his forefinger through the air. "Give me music," he commanded.

I sat on a bench against a wall-sized tapestry of the Last Supper, removed my lute from its case, and set the wood and ivory instrument upon my lap. I began to tune the strings, which lost their tune with every slight change in the weather. When the notes agreed with my ears, I rested my trembling fingers across the six pairs of strings, gathered my breath, then began to play.

Hesitantly, my fingers found their way up the neck of the lute between frets of brass and measured scales. I closed my eyes, trying with all my might to listen to the music, to feel it within myself, and to play it clearly, freely, no matter my fear. And I tried to play, as well as possible, to avoid displeasing the abbot. He held my life in his hands, nearly as did God himself.

When I finished the first song, I paused, waiting to be told to stop, but no such word came. Only the sound of the abbot drinking and eating.

And so I continued, playing songs I had composed at the ruins. I played on, losing myself in the notes. Finally, as I sensed the abbot settling back in his chair, I played the last note, paused, and looked up.

The abbot beamed from his chair and wiped his hand across his mouth. "Play this for young women," he said, throwing his head back with a deep laugh, "and you'll save Cupid a thousand arrows!"

I smiled in return. I had an audience—a grateful audience. The abbot himself.

Clearing his voice, the abbot shifted into a tone as stony, as immovable as the walls. "This gift you have, young man, should be shared . . ."

Perhaps I had found my calling. Suddenly, the idea of working as a blacksmith seemed dull and predictable. It became as clear to me as a blue sky. I'd play my lute, play it from my heart, play it for the enjoyment of others someday.

"Shared here," the abbot continued, "within the house

of God. Here at the monastery. You must listen very carefully to the voice of God and answer his call.

"Go home, pray, and then choose. Talk with your parents and tell them the abbot desires it. I will wait for your reply."

I opened my mouth. When I was eight or nine, I had dreamed of becoming a priest. With each year, that idea had faded steadily and I thought more of living my own life as my father had done. Marrying. And now, the idea of becoming a monk or a priest paled for me. Still, if I were truly being called, as the abbot believed . . .

"You may go now," said the abbot, sitting down.

I began to put my lute away, fumbling with the case. The enormity of what I'd just accomplished made my hands tremble.

I held the case in one hand, the lute in the other, and hurried out of the abbot's banquet room, nearly ran down the corridor, past the chanting in the sanctuary, and finally stood again at the gates under a thick dusting of snowflakes. What strange opportunity was this? To play for the abbot and bury my life in the monastery?

At the gates, which again Brother Augustin opened wide, I left without a word. The young monk slowly closed the monastery gates, and when I looked back, he was still staring, not taking his eyes off me—or more likely, the road beyond.

Under the year's first snowfall, I walked down the empty dirt road. Alone. Free from my brother, free from the walls of the village or the monastery, and filled with more knowledge than my mind could hold. Knowledge of my mother and my father. Knowledge of the ways of the monastery.

I walked faster. To my left, in the distance, the ruins of the Roman fort were washed in a speckled haze of white. Snowflakes steadily fell, showering the bare road and slowly covering up wheel ruts and hoofprints. For a whirling moment, I was tempted to keep walking, to leave everything familiar behind and set off with only my lute on my back.

If the abbot deemed my music worthy of his listening, then others might feel the same way. Visions grew: playing my lute in a bustling village square; strumming before a royal court; wearing the finest leather, the finest boots with shiny silver buckles; playing for beautiful girls and young women. . . . My ideas, like bubbles floating up from the murky bottom of a river, quickly popped.

I knew where my feet would take me. Back to my life, back to my father, back to Jean-Pierre.

By the time I neared the eastern gate of Venyre, my pace slowed. I paused for a few moments and breathed in the air, clean and pure. Ahead, snow lined the village wall. Snow layered everything, turning the world perfectly white, at least on the surface.

THE SMITHY

At dusk, I entered the village with a wave to Celestin, who nodded at me as I passed beneath his watchtower. The street was muddy with patches of white. I walked slowly, as if seeing my village for the first time.

The street leading to my father's shop was quiet, empty, except for the small black dog with the shaggy brown ruff. He was curled in a ball outside the butcher's shop.

"You again?" I said. "Where is everybody?"

The dog whined and thumped his tail. A feathering of snowflakes covered his back. He rose, shook his coat, stretched out his forelegs, and yawned. I reached in my pocket and tossed him a chunk of the monastery bread. He caught it before it hit the ground.

"Good catch," I said, and looked around. The shops were open, but it seemed the villagers had disappeared.

Where was everybody? Had a plague struck? I frowned.

Ahead, my father's blacksmith sign hung crooked, one end broken. The door was wide open. My heart jolted.

Cautiously, I stepped in. "Jean-Pierre? Papa?" I whispered. No answer came in return.

My eyes adjusted to the dimness. The workbench was overturned, the fire had gone out, and the small bench was knocked into another corner on its side. Gaping open, my father's wooden chest revealed parchment—ripped into shreds.

"Papa," I said under my breath.

I searched the shadows, turned in circles, then hovered for a moment in the doorway. Finally, I fled the smithy, tripping over the back of the small dog, which yelped and skittered away. "Out of my way," I snapped. I sprinted toward the sounds erupting from the village square.

As I neared, voices grew into a chorus of mockery: "Huguenots! Huguenots!"

I tucked myself beside the weaver's shop and pretended to take interest in the bright red fabric laid out before me. I had to stop to catch my breath and gather my thoughts. Did someone else know that my father had been reading books? Had he been turned in by a villager? Or did this all have to do with Jean-Pierre?

Two village women turned from the crowd and began walking toward me, heads nearly touching as they talked. They paused near the fabric.

" . . . stormed Marguerite's shop," one of the women said, "and threw everything around, until someone shouted to search the blacksmith's shop. Emanuel Poyet stood by his door while Monsieur Dubois shouted at him, 'Father of the *loup garou*!'"

"Then what happened?" asked the other woman.

I barely breathed and gripped an edge of fabric between my fingers, rubbing it like a baby blanket.

"Emanuel shouted back that there was no such thing."

I closed my eyes, listening.

"Then a soldier said, 'What? He doesn't believe in the *loup garou*? That goes against the Church itself!' At that, they stormed his shop. They must not have found what they were looking for, because the mercenary said the blacksmith was to be held for questioning. But now Monsieur Poyet cannot be found."

"And the child?" the other woman asked.

"Why, he disappeared with his father," came the reply.

"Disappeared?" the woman whispered. "I hate to think . . . with Christmas Eve so close. Maybe they disappeared using some sort of magic. His wife was strange enough—"

"I'm sure they fled and must be hiding," said the other, and their voices faded to nothing as they left the fabrics and walked on.

I tried to swallow. My father had always attended mass, ate fish instead of meat on fast days and closed his smithy to business on Church holidays. Now, as a suspected heretic, he would be the Church's enemy. I clenched fabric in my fists and hung my head.

At my feet, a mottled pigeon pecked at the ground. My own life—my whole future—was no better than this pigeon's. My family was tainted. Before long, I would be no better than the ragged beggars in the square every morning. The abbot's offer—I would have to consider it, even if it meant leaving Jean-Pierre to watch out for himself. And yet, I knew deep within that I couldn't do that either. Not yet. With all my heart I hoped Papa and Jean-Pierre had fled to a place of safety. If so, what if I never saw them again? I suddenly ached with loneliness.

Then I realized someone was sitting in the shadows on the other side of the fabrics, watching. Madame Negrel. The most gossipy, chatty person in all of the village. "Marius," she croaked, "a pity about your father, but don't cry for him. If you're smart, you'll get as far away from him as possible, unless you are cursed as well. As Father Arnaud says, 'We must rid the village of the devil's work.'"

I didn't bother to meet her cloudy, nearly blind eyes. I'd heard more than my mind could absorb. I pivoted away from her, and walked closer toward the crowd gathered in the square. Across from the fountain, behind a leafless tree, I paused, pressing my hand against the tree's grayish-green bark. Suddenly, a wet nose nuzzled my right hand.

I glanced down and rested my hand on the dog's head. His presence, slight as it was, brought me a trace of comfort. Keeping my eyes on the square, I reached into my pocket and gave him the rest of my bread.

The crowd was focused on something in front of a tavern. I caught a glimpse of a soldier beside the caged prisoners, who appeared more like mounds of shriveled leather than men. The soldier, face square and deeply scarred, held a flask to the sky in toast with the mercenary. "May we add to the number of heretics!" he yelled.

Cheering rose from the crowd.

The two men drew their swords, and while hanging on to their mugs, began to fence. The crowd laughed and cheered as steel clashed against steel.

I scanned the crowd for my father, for Jean-Pierre. I edged from behind the tree and paused near a cluster of village men.

"Catherine de Médici—niece to the pope," said one.

"No veering from the Church with her in Paris," said another, "and her fifteen-year-old son as our new king."

"Yes, and thank God her husband, Henry, was killed in that joust last summer," said the third. "He spent our country into ruin! With taxes what they are, we can barely survive."

"The Huguenots have something there," whispered the first. "Optional tithing, less money sent to Rome. Might leave a bit more in my pocket. "

"Shh! You could be burned for such talk—even if it's true."

"With the way my children are growing, my wife will have to start cooking up stray dogs soon." The men laughed.

I cared little about the politics and religion of Paris and the Royal Court. Still, I felt somewhat encouraged to know my father was not the only villager who held startling beliefs. I kept my head down, until the edge of my lute bumped against something.

A woman wider than an ox spun on me.

"Trying to steal from me?" she shouted. Her face was dirty and deeply pitted. She was one of the lucky few to have survived smallpox, but she was grievously ugly to look upon.

"No, Madame," I replied, and tried to slip away from notice.

I glanced ahead at the mercenary, his muscles tightening

in his face. "These prisoners have need for nothing," he shouted, "except the Church's forgiveness! Anyone taking an interest in freeing these men—even offering them a drink—will find his throat slit by morning."

I moved through the crowd swiftly.

"You there!"

"That's the blacksmith's son," a shaggy-browed man said as I passed.

"The blacksmith," said another. "Father of the *loup garou*? Ha! Emanuel Poyet must be the devil himself."

My face flared with heat and I spun around. "My father is no such—" I wanted to find whoever had spoken those words, but when I glanced back, the mercenary, now standing on the wagon's wooden seat, mug lifted high, sword unsheathed, was watching me like a falcon.

JEAN-PIERRE

Trying to not draw attention to myself, I slipped away past the gallows on the edge of the square, up one street, down another, then bounded through the archway and up the stairs, three at a time, to my home.

Madame Troubène was still in bed, her head turned toward me, eyes closed. She was murmuring. I rushed to her side and placed my hand on her forehead, hot as fire. "The pain—" she moaned.

"Where is Jean-Pierre?" I stroked her forehead lightly.

"We can hide him," she managed, "but that won't stop the curse." She raised her trembling hand and pointed toward the stone wall. I had nearly forgotten the place for hiding Jean-Pierre. Years ago, my father had chiseled out a large stone from the wall, right next to a support beam.

I left her bedside, walked over, found the rough edge of mortar and the hairline crack. I knelt, gripped the large stone, eased it out from the wall, and found Jean-Pierre.

He was tucked into a tight ball, head on his knees in the cramped space. He looked up awkwardly, his eyes red, his cheeks tear-streaked.

A breath of relief rushed from my chest.

His lower lip trembled as he opened his mouth. "They . . ." His shoulders shook. "At Papa's shop . . . they threw everything around. I was so scared. But see?" He edged out of his tiny cave, his hair salted with mortar. "You always find me."

I brushed his hair with my fingers. "You're right, Jean-Pierre. I always find you."

"Why did they come in?" he asked, on the verge of tears. "Because of me?"

I avoided his question. "Right now, you must help me. Where's Papa?" I asked.

Jean-Pierre looked around the room. I followed his upward gaze. The chickens ruffled their feathers, clucked, then settled again. "He was up there, but now he's gone."

I knew things were not good, if my father had to hide in the rafters of our home. "Did he say anything?"

I turned to Madame Troubène. "Did he say when he would be back, where he had gone?"

She swallowed and winced, as if she had gravel in her throat. Her eyes were closed and sunken. She spoke, her lips chalky white. "I know nothing."

I ran my hand through my hair. Nothing in my twelve years had prepared me for this. "If only I could ask him . . . What am I supposed to do?"

Jean-Pierre tugged on the edge of my rope belt. "Where's Papa?"

I didn't know what to say. I walked to the shutters, opened them, and looked out. The street was dark, the air frozen. I quickly closed the shutters.

I poured a mug of water from the pitcher, drank deeply, then wiped my mouth. I walked around the room, then slumped against the door.

"I don't know, Jean-Pierre."

"Is it because of me?" Jean-Pierre looked steadily into my eyes. "Is it because I'm a *loup garou*, as everyone says?"

People had always whispered, but I thought that I had kept their rumors from Jean-Pierre. Of course, I couldn't protect him from the village talk forever. I held the mug out to Jean-Pierre, who took it in his small hands and drained it.

"See? Even the child knows," came Madame Troubène's voice. "The wolves have been howling at night . . . calling him."

I jumped from my knees and stood. "No!" I said. "That's not true!" I combed my fingers through my hair and paced.

"When I carried Jean-Pierre back in my arms, it's true, the wolves had been howling, but I didn't see a single wolf as I returned to the village. If Jean-Pierre was truly being called, then why hasn't he changed shape by now?" My voice grew louder. "Jean-Pierre hurt himself, that's all! The wolves were calling to one another. Nothing more. You know what I think? I think perhaps there is no *loup garou*, none at all."

I suddenly froze. To say this thought out loud. Not to believe in the *loup garou* was . . . was by itself heresy.

Jean-Pierre had crunched himself into a little ball

against the wall, his arms wrapped around his knees, head tucked down. "I want Papa," he said.

My own limbs trembled, but I knelt beside my brother and touched his cheek. "Look at me."

Jean-Pierre slowly lifted his head. Tears brimmed in his eyes. "Beautiful, haunting eyes," my father had said of my mother. Jean-Pierre's were just like hers, framed with thick lashes.

"Listen to me," I said. I lifted my brother's chin. I met his eyes and held them. "You're Jean-Pierre."

His chin puckered, then quivered. "But the people were shouting, Marius. Even Madame Troubène believes . . ."

I tried to smile. "Who is with you every day?"

"You."

"And am I afraid of you?"

Jean-Pierre wiped his eyes with his small fist. Still they filled with tears. He shook his head.

"That's because you're my brother. And all that other talk is foolishness."

"Careful," croaked Madame Troubène from her bed. "That talk is trouble . . ." She breathed hard. "You should know . . ." she managed, then fell silent.

I held Jean-Pierre's gaze and squeezed his shoulders. "You must promise me two things. First, that you'll stay close to me. You must not go running off. Second, if anyone asks you, 'Are you the *loup garou?*' you say, 'No, I'm Jean-Pierre.' Do you understand?"

Jean-Pierre didn't say anything. "But why . . . why do I . . ."

"Promise me," I said sternly, sounding almost like my father.

Jean-Pierre blinked his large deer eyes. "I promise, Marius," he whispered.

"Good. Now we must get some sleep. Tomorrow will come quickly."

I led Jean-Pierre to our shared mattress. I covered him with the thin blanket, then turned and walked to the window. For just a moment, I opened the shutters again, and peered out.

Like goose feathers, snow was falling again.

I shivered and began to close the shutters. As I did, eerily, on the breeze came the distant sound of wolves howling. One cry, then two, then countless more. Their song caught in my chest. I waited. Their howling lasted a short time, then dropped away into the silence from which their song had come.

I hoped I was right about Jean-Pierre. God above, I hoped I was. *Morning.* I would focus on that. Everything would be better in the morning. I'd find my father, and I would find a way to keep Jean-Pierre safe. A plan. At the first streak of light, I wanted to be the only one on the streets of Venyre.

My Father

I woke in the middle of the night to Madame Troubène's coughing. She was in her bed, lying on her side, with a cough that seemed to shake the whole room.

The fire that I'd stoked to roaring before going to bed was nearly out. Reluctantly, I rose from the warmth of my mattress, dressed quickly, and added a few logs to the flickering embers.

Jean-Pierre still slept soundly. My father's mattress lay in the opposite corner, empty.

Quietly, I slipped out into the night and tiptoed down the stairs to the street. I clung to the shadows of our arched entrance. Moonlight spilled like fresh milk into the streets and lit up thin patches of snow. From the far end of a street, muffled sounds floated from the tavern. Otherwise, the village was quiet.

If my father was anywhere in Venyre, he had to be in

his smithy. I touched the cool iron door handle, turned it, and stepped in. "Papa?" I whispered.

"Close the door, Marius," came a familiar voice, "and bolt it." All the anger, all the resentment I'd felt earlier on this threshold vanished. Relief washed over me.

The room was dark until my father lit a candle. The flame illuminated his worry-filled eyes, his bearded face. Still, he smiled. "Marius," he said and reached for me.

"I hoped to find you here," I said.

"I couldn't let thieves steal my tools without a fight."

I hugged my father tightly, breathed in the smoky smell of his hair, and welcomed his scratchy beard against my forehead.

My father stepped back and brought the candle between us. "I must meet with the others," he said. "There is much to tell, but precious little time."

"Brother Gabriel told me," I whispered. "He said you can read."

My father, with a distant gaze, looked past me. I wished I could see into his thoughts, understand what lay behind his shadowed eyes. Then a brief smile played on his face, and I saw something there. A glint of pride.

"Yes," he said. "It's true. And reading is only the start. Books lead to learning, and learning leads to knowing more than . . ." He paused and glanced toward the door. "More than the Church would have a simple man like me know. Indulgences, for instance. Paying your way into heaven. It's rubbish."

To hear him speak so boldly, so defiantly . . . My blood quickened.

"Do you want to know what the Bible does say?"

I waited, not sure I wanted to know. This talk scared me.

"It says: 'And what does the Lord require of you, but to do justice, to love mercy, and to walk humbly with your God.' Simple enough for a goat to understand."

My father had never spoken so boldly, or so much. I suddenly felt awkward. "Why . . . why did they destroy your shop? Is that why you had me take the books?"

"Yes. But even without the books, they found parchment—with my writing on it. But they couldn't ruin everything," he said. "My tools are sound. When we get resettled, I will be back to my trade."

"But what of . . . are you . . . a Huguenot?"

My father looked at me. The candle's flame danced in the darkness. He rested a hand on my shoulder. "I aim to be a free man, Marius. To think for myself, to pray to God by myself, to pray in French, to read whatever I wish . . . and if these actions make me a Huguenot, then so be it. God knows I am not alone."

I leaned on my father's confidence. I suddenly felt drawn, as if to a fire's warmth. And at the same time, as in tales from the coast, I felt as if I were following him to the end of a ship's plank, about to fall into fatal waters.

"You're trembling," said my father. He removed his hand from my shoulder, cupped it around the candle's flame, and blew it out. "We don't want to attract attention," he said. "As soon as possible, when the time is right, you and Jean-Pierre and I will leave Venyre."

"Leave?" This news was too much. "Venyre is our home," I said. "And Madame Troubène . . . she's old, and . . . like a storm, all that has happened will blow by . . . and we can stay here and—"

"Marius." My father's tone was true as a bowman's arrow. "This is what I meant when I said the times are not what they seem. Many of us, we live like rats between the walls, afraid of the rat catcher. It's not the way to live."

Tears pooled hot in my eyes. *Everything.* It was everything on top of everything. I swallowed and cleared my throat. "I knew you married Mama for love. But why did you never tell me that she was from nobility?"

"Would knowing the truth have helped?" my father answered. Then his voice grew lighter. "Would it have helped you escape the taunts of that fat, sniveling butcher who should keep his nose in his own business?"

I laughed. He'd never called Monsieur Dubois "fat" and "sniveling" before. "No, I suppose not."

"You've had enough to carry on your shoulders with your brother's curse," he said. "And not a curse due to the hour of his birth—or by the full moon—but cursed instead by the ignorance, superstition, and fear of his own neighbors. The only monstrosities I see in Venyre are our own cruelties to one another."

"Then . . . you don't believe he's . . ."

I felt my father's hand on my head, heavy and strong. "Your brother is as good, as true, as the love your mother and I shared."

I bowed my head. "I feel as if all of Jean-Pierre's life . . ." I struggled to find the right words. "I feel I have betrayed him, along with everyone else, by fearing him . . . by doubting his goodness."

"Ah, but that same goodness is solidly in you, Marius.

And that's why we must leave. I don't want you to live like a rat, picking crumbs from the nobleman's or the abbot's table. Your heart is good, your mind is quick. A blacksmith's life is a good life, especially if you take pride in your craft. But I want more for you than to stay in Venyre where learning is something to be feared."

"The abbot," I blurted, remembering that I indeed had choices, that I wasn't stuck, "he heard me play the lute . . ."

"The abbot? He noticed your gift?"

I nodded.

"He heard your mother play here in the village—just once—and from that moment forward, your uncle Gabriel and she made sure the abbot never knew they were related."

"Why?"

"The less Abbot Joseph knows, the better. He is a man who thrives on power, and will twist whatever he can to fulfill his own wants and desires. Avoid him. Soon we'll leave for a place where you will be free to learn to read and write. To think for yourself. That's my dream for you—your mother's dream as well."

Suddenly, a soft knock, just once, then twice, came at the door.

"You and I—at least we're not alone in this," my father said with a wry smile. "Many, many others share our views. Now I must go and meet with a few of them. And you—you must return to Jean-Pierre and keep him hidden."

He embraced me fiercely, then unbolted the door and whispered, "I'll come for you. Soon."

Then my father stepped onto the snowy street, and along with two other caped shadows, disappeared around the street corner into the deep night.

I stole home to the warmth of my bed.

Wolf-Tooth Necklace

December 23

At dawn, when light was only a shade above darkness, I climbed out of bed. Had I merely dreamed that I'd seen my father? My mind ran over our conversation the way a tongue explores the hole from a missing tooth. No, the entire encounter had been real. My father had talked more to me last night than he had in my whole life. The gap I'd felt between us for so many years was closing.

I yanked on my breeches and jerkin and walked lightly past Madame Troubène.

"Marius," she croaked, and reached for my arm. "You've been like my own son. Your mother," she began, then started wheezing hard, her lungs struggling for air, "she would be so proud of you."

I kissed her forehead, which was icy, deathly cold. "What can I do to help?"

"Go to the apothecary," she said. "Get something for

78

the pain. Take my money," she said, so softly that I had to lean closer to her mouth as she spoke, "what little there is . . . in the chest."

In the cedar chest at the foot of her bed were table-cloths, mugs, and jars of spices and herbs, as well as a small leather pouch. I slipped her pouch inside my belted tunic, not bothering to count its contents.

"I'll hurry," I said and left.

Outside, a flock of snow geese flew soundlessly over-head, white against gray, heading south toward the Mediterranean. They took turns in flight, the lead bird dropping back as another bird took the front, acting as a windbreak for the others. I breathed in the icy air and made my way through a covering of snow, choosing my steps carefully, not wanting to fall in dung again.

The streets were quiet, windows shuttered, merchants' booths covered until full daylight.

"*Bonjour*, Marius," came a voice from across the street. The butcher's.

I nearly leaped out of my jerkin.

"Did you hear about your papa?" asked Monsieur Dubois, uncovering the meats at his shop. Then he faced me and rubbed his hands over and over on his apron, al-most gleefully.

"That they stormed his shop without cause?" I said an-grily. "Yes, I heard."

"Oh, now you have your tongue," he said with a chuckle. "And how is Madame Troubène? I haven't seen her in days. Did she, too, simply disappear? Strange things going on at your home."

"She's fallen ill. I'm on my way to the apothecary now," I said.

"Too bad about your father," called the butcher. "If you should see him, warn him to be more careful. These are dangerous times."

I quickened my steps, rounded a corner, and walked halfway down the street. At the apothecary's sign, I knocked on the door and waited for an answer. It finally came in the form of a man in skullcap and rumpled clothes who stood no taller than my chin.

"What can be so important this early?"

"Madame Troubène," I said. "I think she's dying." And as soon as I spoke the words, the weight of what I had not wanted to admit struck me. She had given me her money, something she usually guarded like a dog with its bone. She had told me I was like her own son, when she was usually rather gruff and stingy with her affection.

"She's in pain," I said, and my voice cracked. "She needs something powerful that will make her sleep better." Suddenly, I had in mind that I'd give Jean-Pierre some of the medicine, as well, should anyone search the house again. Then he could remain perfectly quiet, in hiding.

"Right now she is lying very still and very cold."

"She should be bled," said the wiry man. "Talk to the barber as soon as he opens." He began to close his door with a yawn.

I had seen the barber's special blades, used both for cutting hair and beards, and also for letting out bad blood. Sometimes bowls of it sat beneath a customer's chair. "But she's very weak. She can't get out of her bed. I don't think—"

"If she is unable to get there," the apothecary continued, his eyes wide as an owl's, "the barber may be persuaded to come to her bed and bleed her there. For the right fee."

"Is there something else? Something you could give her?"

The apothecary yawned again, then stepped backward. He opened the door to his shop. "I can see you're not easily put off. Come in then."

He lit a tallow candle, and in the dimness I made out small shelves filled with various lidded containers, mortars and pestles, hanging herbs, vials of various sizes, and slatted wooden barrels on the floor. The apothecary, his cloak draped over his sleep shirt, reached over to a tile and board where small, round gray objects had been rolled out and left to dry.

"This is something of my own creation," he said. "Only just yesterday did I use my mortar and pestle to create a paste, a powerful medicine, which I then rolled into these shapes."

I tried to act interested. "Oh, yes. Amazing."

"Medicine pebbles, that's what I'll call them," he said proudly.

Hands covered with sores, he picked up a handful of the gray pebbles, found a tiny wooden box, and put them inside.

"Tell her to place one of these under her tongue. It will dissolve slowly and she'll sleep. She'll feel no pain whatsoever." He handed me the box.

I tucked it in my pocket along with the remaining monastery bread. "Perfect," I said.

"I'm not finished," he said, then began to rummage through his shop, his candle rising and falling as he searched high and low.

I waited.

"Ah, here it is," he finally said. He turned to me with a leather necklace, from which dangled a long wolf's tooth coiled securely in wire. "And you. You should wear this for your own protection." He paused, his wide eyes searching mine.

I nodded, and despite my bold words to Jean-Pierre, a tremor traveled through me.

"Tomorrow is Christmas Eve," he said. "The werewolves will gather, and this year we will have a full moon, as well. The powers of darkness will be greater than ever. Keep a close eye on . . ." He let his words hang there. "Never, never remove the necklace."

Despite my strong words yesterday and my father's reassurance that the *loup garou* did not exist, I hesitated. My stomach turned with the weight of a millstone. I took the necklace, put it around my neck, and slipped it beneath my shirt.

The white tooth felt cold against my bare skin, and strangely, brought me relief. I did not believe in the *loup garou*, yet the necklace made me feel more secure. I could not figure out my own mind.

"Pay attention," the apothecary said, his forefinger poised in the air. "Have you found a special salve? The *loup garou* uses a salve, given by the devil to help it change from a human into a *loup garou* and back again. Have you seen anything like that lying around?"

I shook my head.

"Even so, a *loup garou* is cunning. It takes a quick wit to identify one. For example, I'm sure you heard of the nobleman who was out hunting in the woods. He caught a wolf, cut off its paw, wrapped it in cloth strips, and returned to his chateau. When he returned, he found his wife in bed, her hand in a bandage. The nobleman unwrapped the wolf's paw," the apothecary said, dramatizing the story with his sore-covered hands, "but instead found it was his wife's hand, complete with her wedding ring. The woman was tried and burned at the stake."

My stomach turned at his story. I must have made a disagreeable face.

"It's a true story," he said. "You wear that necklace."

The apothecary cleared his throat, stated the amount due, and held out his hand for payment. I reached into m' money purse for Madame Troubène's money. By the time had finished counting out the *deniers*, the purse was nea empty. *"Merci,"* I said, and quickly left the darkness o shop.

At the mill, which was just opening, a women wa ing bread. I bought a loaf, tucked it beneath my a raced home. As I rounded my street corner, the cresting the village walls. Ice-covered puddles Pigeons swooped over the village, ready to sear st day for crumbs. be

By the time I returned, Madame Troub g, a asleep. For her sake, I was glad she wouldr "I've bled. Not yet, at least. She did not like e had treatment she feared. "In all my years," seen as many die as live in the hands of b a good one in our village, that might be

Jean-Pierre lay on his back, snoring softly, his mouth open wide enough to catch a team of horses. "Wake up," I whispered, and shook his shoulder.

He squeezed his eyes shut tighter, groaned, and rolled toward the wall. I tossed back the blanket, pulled him from his sleep, and stood him on his feet. "First, use the pot." I handed him the night pot.

Jean-Pierre mumbled and stared into it as if he'd never seen it before.

"Then," I continued, "you must go back into hiding . . ."

"But I don't want to . . ." he whined, something he rarely did.

I pulled the loaf of bread out from behind my back. "And you may eat this." I broke it in half. "The other half *is for Papa, as soon as I find him." I would not tell Jean-*erre about last night. Not yet. I had no idea how long it *uld be until our father came for us.

*hen I removed the box of medicine from my pocket *ut a round pebble in my brother's palm. "If I'm not *nd someone comes up the stairs, put one of these* beneath your tongue. It will help you sleep and *el nothing at all."

*lr, Madame Troubène moaned. I stepped to her *n your mouth, please," I said, suddenly feeling *her.

pebb* her lips cracked and dry.

"N*tongue." She did and I placed a medicine *She* it.

kissed h*

*n response, never opening her eyes. I *d, her skin cold beneath my lips.

84

When Jean-Pierre was done with the night pot, he crawled into his small cave in the wall with half the loaf. I slid the stone into place, restoked the fire, and started down the stairs.

Before I reached the archway, Marguerite met me, her face pale and drawn. Years, it seemed, had passed since I had cupped my hands before her at the well two days earlier.

"Marius," she said, placing her hand on mine. "Last night . . . your father . . ." She bit her lower lip and closed her eyes.

I waited, knowing in my soul this wasn't good news she carried. So Marguerite was one of the caped figures who had met with my father last night. She had often stitched beside my mother. Perhaps Mama had taught her to read, as well.

Marguerite glanced over her shoulder, then brought her face closer to mine and whispered, "The mercenaries arrested him early this morning. We were gathering in secret. Your father was sharing, talking about what he had read in the Bible when they burst through the doors." Her mouth quivered. "They should have taken me as well."

"Where is he now?" I asked.

"The guardhouse."

"Isn't there something we can do?" I asked.

She closed her eyes tightly, then opened them. "God knows I'm praying for an answer." She sighed deeply. "They arrested him for heresy."

Then she turned, and I followed down the last steps after her.

At the street, she abruptly pulled her cape over her

scooped blouse and vest, and over her dark hair and white heart-shaped cap. "Marius, please understand," she said, "even if you're told he's evil—your father is no such thing. He is a good man, Marius. A brave man."

Then, hoisting her skirts above the snow and mud, she quickly walked away, head high.

HOUSE TO HOUSE

A rooster crowed from a rooftop as the sun rose higher over the horizon. Somehow, I had to talk to my father.

"Marius," Monsieur Dubois called from across the street. He stepped from his boucherie and met me midway, his eyebrows furrowed behind a teasing smile. "You want to find your father?"

I didn't answer.

"Father Arnaud has decided justice can be served just as well here in Venyre, rather than cart the men all the way to Avignon."

I had heard plenty about Avignon. A papal city, home to numerous bishops, and filled with cathedrals, monasteries, and chapels. Maybe justice would be less harsh in Venyre than in Avignon.

"And a good thing, too," Monsieur Dubois continued. He crossed his arms and placed his hands beneath his armpits. "We need a reminder here of the power of the Church. We need a deep cleansing from time to time."

"My father," I said. "What will they do to him?"

"The prisoners are locked up, to be tortured," the butcher said matter-of-factly.

Torture. I closed my eyes.

"The clergy will get their confessions of heresy. They always have. They always do."

"But . . . Not my father! He's done nothing wrong. He's a good man."

"That's not for you to decide, Marius." The butcher rested his flabby hand on the top of my head. "Perhaps this is true justice at last," he said.

I slapped away his hand.

"Your father always thought he was too good for the rest of us. Started to question everything like an outsider."

I crossed my arms over my chest. "You don't know anything about my father." He can read, I wanted to say, he knows as much as any priest, but I held my tongue.

"I know this," the butcher said. "Your mother, an unusual woman, kept too much to herself. And your father—he was blind to her oddness, completely taken by her." His words came faster and spittle formed at the corners of his mouth. "He and I grew up friends, right here on this street. He went away, in search of greater opportunities as an artisan, but when he returned from his travels with her, she had clearly cast a spell over him. He bowed to her, wasn't man enough to put her in her place. He could never see beyond her beauty, but I could. I saw she wasn't like other women, all those fancy words, her way of charming with the lute."

I opened my mouth, ready to defend my mother, but held back, letting the butcher ramble.

"She was a tool of the devil, if ever there was one."

"No, she was—"

The butcher lunged toward me, his face too close to mine, his breath vile. "She died," he whispered, "before anyone could test her. I know, if she'd been thrown into the deep bend of the river, I'd trade anyone an ox that she would have come up swimming, proof enough that she was"—he spat out the last words—"a witch!"

"And if she'd drowned, then what?" I'd heard this logic before.

"Well, then at least your father would have come to his senses and started acting like a *man*." Drops of spittle hit my cheek. "But she didn't live long enough to be put to the test. Just long enough to leave behind a cursed child. I'm not blind, not like your father."

I stood my ground. "You know nothing about my mother or my father. Better people than you'll ever be! All you do is pry into people's lives, turning over stones to find whatever you can." Heat flared up the back of my neck. I knew I was forgetting my place. I could be flogged for speaking to an adult this way. "You—you're a fat, sniveling pig—scared of your own shadow!"

The butcher lunged, hands toward my neck.

I leaped away and bolted down the street.

I rounded a corner into the square, where my father had more than once studied placards handed out by travelers. Studied them longer than most. Now I knew he had been *reading* the words.

Donkeys pulled carts and merchants set up boards

filled with squash and carrots, salted and smoked fish, pork sausage of every kind, herbs, and oils. Today, it seemed, neither the panic about heretics nor last night's snowfall would keep them, or the sun, away.

I darted behind a wagonload of bright fabrics, headed past the tavern where the wagon of caged men had been yesterday. They were gone. They, too, were likely imprisoned at the guardhouse across the square, the large stone building just beyond the gallows.

I neared the building. At street level, a rat scurried through one of the grated windows to the space below, where prisoners were bound by chains to the walls. More than once, I had walked by and looked down, catching a glimpse of prisoners.

I couldn't look in. I'd stood up to the butcher who had tormented me and my brother for years, but what did that matter in light of my father's fate? Torture. The thought nearly broke me. My energy drained as I drew closer and squatted beside a window. I wove my fingers into the cast-iron grate.

"Papa?" I called softly down. "Papa, are you down there?"

All was shadow below, and despite the damp, chilly air, a smell as foul as dead, bloated rats struck me. I clamped my hand across my nose.

"Marius." My father's voice floated up from somewhere below. "Marius, if anyone sees you . . ."

"No talking among yourselves!" shouted a much stronger voice.

I huddled closer. My thin shoes were soaked from running in the streets. I began to shiver violently.

Moments passed. Finally, my father whispered, "Take care of your brother, and of yourself. I'm in God's hands now."

"Enough!" came the soldier's voice. "You, who are you speaking to out there?"

I sprang to my feet and darted away. I tore between carts, nearly tipping over a stack of woven baskets. A woman cursed me as I passed.

Beside the church, I slowed, eyeing the side entrance door, then stepped into the silence. If ever I had needed a miracle, now was the time. I paused at the stone font, dipped my fingers in the cold holy water, then made the sign of the cross with the tips of my fingers, touching my forehead, my pounding chest, my left shoulder, and then my right.

Thatched wooden chairs sat empty in neat, straight lines. For hundreds and hundreds of years, the Church had ruled; now people like my father were challenging its authority. I hesitated, unsure of my place within its walls. Should I even step inside to pray? Yet, if God was God, what did it matter? And if God was love, surely He would hear my plea for help. Help for a good father. Help for myself.

Tiers of candles, a few lit and burning, edged the sanctuary. I knelt before them. "Lord God," I whispered, "I pray for my father. May you keep him."

I didn't know what else to say. I rose, closed my eyes with a deep breath, and suddenly felt the presence of someone beside me. A sense that I wasn't alone.

I opened my eyes and without moving my body, looked left and right. No one was there. I turned around slowly. I was completely alone in the sanctuary.

A shiver passed through me. Had I sensed an angel? I closed my eyes again. The spicy, smoky, sweet smell of incense lingered from an earlier mass. My heart beat louder in my ears than any other sound. But the sensation was gone.

The presence hadn't been my imagination. I had felt it the way I had when my mother had been alive and was nearby. Perhaps it was a sign, just for me, that my prayers would be answered, even if I hadn't prayed in Latin as the priests did. I opened my eyes again and walked down the aisle, my damp soles sticking on smooth marble.

I reached the heavy side door, pushed hard, and eased outside. Sunlight glared off patches of snow. The clatter of hoofbeats grew louder, coming toward me. To my left I saw the abbot, riding his white-starred black horse. As he drew near, I ran to his side.

"Abbot Joseph!" I made the sign of the cross. Here was an immediate answer to my prayer.

The horse didn't slow.

"My father," I said in a rush, running alongside the abbot, "has been falsely arrested!" Though Brother Gabriel and my father had both warned me about the abbot, I hoped I had won a small measure of favor in his eyes. I had a chance. "There's talk of torture and heresy. Please, please, help him, I beg you!"

Abbot Joseph looked down absently, his red-splotched forehead stern, his jowls loose in his face. Then his eyes brightened. He pulled his horse to a stop. "Oh, the lute player. Have you made your decision then? I'm waiting to hear you play."

"I—I wasn't asking to play," I said, catching my wind.

"My father has been falsely arrested. There's been a mistake!"

The abbot turned away and looked straight ahead. "Talk to me only when you have something to say. Something I want to hear. Of course, I could require you to play your lute, but I prefer that it be your own choice. You'll play better then." He lifted his horse's reins and galloped into the square.

I followed at a distance, slowly. What kind of man of God was this? He had no heart at all. Only his own will, his own wants guiding him. He didn't care a speck for my concerns or for my father.

As the abbot reached the center of the square, a crowd began to form beside the fountain. Soon, several priests assembled. A trumpeter blew his horn, drawing in a larger and larger audience. I waited, glancing toward the guardhouse.

Soon, the crowd quieted, and the parish priest, Father Arnaud, took his place beside the abbot and announced: "Today, in the village of Venyre, the Church makes a plea." He held his arms wide. "This is the day to uproot all evil, to bring all heretics, witches, werewolves, and workers of sorcery to justice before Holy Christmas Day. Evil is spreading across France. It has too long lingered beneath our roofs, causing a stench to reach God Himself. Yesterday," he said, sweeping his palm over the crowd, "yesterday was a beginning. Today the Church will prevail. All who know of neighbors cavorting with the devil, defying the ways and doctrine of the Church, must step forward now. To hold your tongue is to sin against God Almighty."

Murmuring passed through the crowd, then individuals began to step forward, one by one.

The peasant woman with the basket of chickens limped forward. I noticed her basket was empty. "My chickens were alive when I came here," she said, wagging her finger at the crowd, "but now they're dead. All of them! Someone here put a curse on them!"

I didn't want to linger. I started to walk backward, to get as far away from this kind of neighbor-against-neighbor justice as I could. Suddenly, I felt a familiar, thick hand grab my forearm. I glanced over my shoulder. It was Monsieur Dubois.

He yanked me off my feet and dragged me like a pig to the front of the crowd, right beneath the nose of the abbot.

"This one," said the butcher. "His father, we know, has already been arrested for Huguenot activity, for going against the teachings of the Holy Church. And to add to the suspicion, only this morning he bought himself a wolf-tooth necklace from our own apothecary." Monsieur Dubois grabbed the necklace from beneath my jerkin, lifted the cord in his fist, and let the tooth dangle white in the sunlight.

I gasped, choking, and struggled to get away. "Father Arnaud, Abbot Joseph," the butcher continued, "Marius is afraid of his own brother, who everyone knows was born on Christmas Eve. Why wait for his brother to grow old enough to tear out someone's heart? Already we struggle enough. This family will only bring more curses upon Venyre!"

Then the butcher let go of me. I fell forward, stumbling, but managed to stay on my feet.

"We will start a search," Father Arnaud said. "And we will begin at the home of Marius Poyet." He met my eyes. "I promise, with God's help, to determine whether the devil is at work in your brother."

I held the priest's gaze. Once, I'd wished to serve as his altar boy. Now I turned away.

"From there," Abbot Joseph announced, standing taller than Father Arnaud, "we will conduct a house-to-house search of the entire village. We will leave no stone unturned."

Under my breath, one name slipped soundlessly from my lips: "Jean-Pierre."

THE CROWD

Reluctantly, I led Father Arnaud, several soldiers, and curious villagers down the street I'd known forever, passed the battered sign of my father's shop, then paused at the archway leading to my home. My heart pounded.

"But Madame Troubène," I said, trying to stall the search, "she's ill and it would disturb her too much if—"

"Ill? You lead the way then," Father Arnaud said, with a hint of fear behind his command.

I took the stairs slowly, one step at a time, clearing my throat, trying to make as much noise as possible, but no matter how hard I stepped, my leather shoes were quiet on the stones. I hoped to give Jean-Pierre some warning that we were coming. He could take the medicine pebble. Madame Troubène, despite her own worries, still loved Jean-Pierre. She, I hoped, would make sure he stayed hidden.

I pushed open the door. "Sorry, Madame—I brought

visitors. . . ." I spoke loudly, hoping Jean-Pierre would hear.

"*Bonjour*, Madame," announced the priest. "Forgive us for disturbing you, but your home must be searched."

Madame Troubène lay still on her bed. A crucifix had fallen from her grip and lay on her chest.

I feared she was dead. The room was icy still. I stepped closer and placed my head over her heart. It beat slowly. She barely breathed. I kissed her pale and wrinkled forehead.

The priest swept past me to her bed, studied her face, then turned to the others pouring into the room. "Let's hope this is not the start of God's punishment. Pray it is not the sweats returning to Venyre!"

Whispers of "the sweats" rolled down the stairs from one person to another. Sweating sickness had swept through France when I was a young child, and Venyre had lost many children and old people. Healthy people were even said to have dropped dead in the middle of speaking. In the stairway, some began to whisper "the plague." Maybe this anxiety was what Brother Gabriel had meant about fear like a grass fire. All it took was the right wind, the right word.

I covered Madame Troubène's bare feet with her blanket.

"Where is your brother?" Father Arnaud asked.

I blinked and looked around the room, then shrugged.

"Find the boy," ordered the priest. He grabbed the crucifix lying on Madame Troubène's chest and thrust it at the mercenary. "Search for him. If we wait until Christmas Eve, you may need more than your sword."

I edged toward the stone wall where my brother—I prayed—was still hiding. I gathered my lute, sat down, and began to pluck the strings softly. I played as the wooden chest was emptied: linens, pewter goblets, bowls, and spices fell amid the rushes on the floor.

I strummed as the mercenary thrust his sword over and over again into the straw-filled mattress where Jean-Pierre and I slept every night. I played as soldiers descended the stairs. I closed my eyes and played when all grew silent around me. I played until I heard the house-to-house search move from my street to the next.

I played until sometime late in the sun's course across the sky, played until light turned gray between the cracks in the shutters, played until my fingers felt raw, played until I heard the soft whimpers of Jean-Pierre behind the wall.

Then I eased the stone back. Jean-Pierre's face was ashen, dusty, and tear-streaked. "I wet myself," he said, shaking his head. "I tried to stay still as long as I could."

I grabbed my brother and buried my head in his neck. *"C'est bien,"* I said. "You did just fine." I realized he couldn't stay forever in hiding. Much better to escape to somewhere beyond the reach of village hysteria. *The ruins.* I would take Jean-Pierre there, while it was dark, and wrap him in blankets in the highest tower. I could visit there during the day, and at night perhaps I could return. All I knew was I needed to get my brother as far away from the village as possible. My father had charged me with his welfare. I couldn't let him down. "We must hurry," I said to Jean-Pierre.

Just then, a stir of movement sounded beyond the door.

I jumped toward it, ready to drop the wooden bolt into its casing. How could I have been so forgetful as not to lock it? Before I was halfway across the room, the door inched open and Monsieur Dubois crossed the threshhold, his gaze directed beyond me to Jean-Pierre.

"I knew if I waited long enough," he said, "you'd find each other." A hint of a smile showed beneath his ample lips. He glanced at Madame Troubène, who had slept through it all. The medicine pebble had spared her from this pain.

The butcher brushed past me to Jean-Pierre. "Look at this, bruises on his face. A sure sign, it is, that he was out with the devil himself. Who did you rip open then? Some innocent traveler?"

I pushed myself between Jean-Pierre and the butcher. "Stay away from him! You know nothing!"

The butcher backhanded me and sent me flying to the mattress. "Someone," he said, "must see to it that the boy is locked up before he changes, before the moon climbs higher."

Stunned, I watched Monsieur Dubois tuck Jean-Pierre under his arm and carry him like a young boar to market.

Something told me I might never return to this place. My life was crumbling beneath me. I staggered to my feet, grabbed the lute, and hurried after my brother into the twilight.

TORCHES

A thudding of hooves sounded to my right. I jolted to a stop. A traveler on horseback was heading swiftly toward the eastern gate.

"Please help," I cried, running into the street and nearly throwing myself beneath his horse's hooves.

"Trying to kill yourself?" He was a young man with a slender nose, his beard tucked inside a cloak of the highest quality.

"Please, *monsieur*, I—"

"I would love to help," the young man said with a sweep of his arm, "but I must be on my way."

"This is important," I said, reaching inside my tunic and pulling out my money purse. "I haven't much, but I'll pay you something."

The man pulled on his horse's reins. "I'll listen, for a moment, then I'm leaving this village for towns more hospitable."

"Just this," I said. "Go to St. Benedict's, the monastery to the northwest, and give Brother Gabriel this message: *the fire is out of control.* Will you do this—please—as an act of Christian charity?" I held out a few coins.

"Ah." The man brushed away the offer of money, lifted his reins, and galloped toward the gate. "I wish you well!"

For a second, I stood there, money pouch dangling from my fingertips as I watched the man ride away. Hardly a speck of goodwill could be found anywhere. And where was God in all of this? My belly turned on itself in anger.

I stuffed my money purse back in my tunic and headed toward the village square, where a round sphere of light glowed, soft and beckoning, almost as if something holy and good were taking place in the heart of my village, almost as if God had ordained the house-to-house search.

I ran, and my chest filled sharply with air; with each exhalation my breath formed a misty cloud of white. I remembered the candle I'd lit at church. God, please, add my brother to that prayer. Keep him safe along with my father. Send an angel.

Ahead, in the center of the square, Monsieur Dubois was holding Jean-Pierre over his head. Torchlights glowed, some held high by villagers, others burning from the outside walls of the guardhouse.

"See these bruises?" the butcher called. "It is no coincidence that the night after wolves were howling beyond our walls, this boy is covered with bruises!"

I had heard the talk. Anyone suddenly covered with bruises was believed to have been out at night as a *loup garou*, running with other wolves, attacking sheep, pigs, and people. But not my brother. I knew full well where the bruises had come from. I didn't care what happened to myself; I had to speak out.

"He fell from a high place at the ruins!" I shouted.

A few villagers turned to listen.

"Just a few nights past—we were out and he fell. That's why he has bruises! No other reason!"

"The wolves were howling last night," a woman shouted, somewhere beyond my view. "A legion of werewolves. This child must have been with them!"

The villagers pressed closer to my brother, touching and looking. Exclamations rose from some. "A sure sign!" screeched Madame Negrel, clutching the arm of her aging husband.

I rushed forward. "My brother is not a *loup garou!*"

Someone grabbed my arm and held me fast. I wrestled free.

"Unexplainable!" shouted the butcher. "The only answer is that he was out preying upon victims and has now turned back to this innocent form. But the bruises remain! Now, we must keep him from returning to the forest for his salve. If he cannot get to it, we will be safe."

"The wolves will have their celebration tomorrow. The eve of Christmas," said another. "We must make no room for evil in our midst."

"We have no other way to kill the werewolf in the boy," said the butcher, "other than to burn him at the stake."

"Cut off a limb! An arm, a leg!" called another. "You're the butcher. Then we'll know for sure. If we find a shaggy coat beneath his skin, we'll know the truth. We'll have him!"

The butcher didn't reply.

"Yes, cut off a limb!"

"He may look innocent," said a young woman with a baby clutched tight, pleading in a high voice to those around her, "but that's the devil, tricking us into doing nothing, tricking us into thinking we're safe!"

I was only a breath away from my brother. Jean-Pierre's eyes were wide, whites exposed. Tears streamed down his cheeks, which were pale as ice.

"Please," I cried. "Listen! My brother is good, he isn't evil, he—"

"Just like your father, I suppose you're going to tell us!" someone shouted.

Uneasy laughter rang through the crowd. "Bring him to the guardhouse!"

"Keep us safe! Lock him up for the night!"

"Burn him in the morning with the rest!"

Burn him in the morning with the rest. Was this the fate decided for my father?

Feelings of worthlessness flooded me. I had done nothing of use. Maybe there was nothing I could have done for Papa, but I'd tried to help Jean-Pierre. My efforts had only made things worse. I might just as well have delivered Jean-Pierre into the hands of the crowd all on my own. As if my head were suddenly full of feathers, my vision became foggy. My stomach turned sour, and I bent at the waist, hands to my knees. I felt as if I were spinning, faster and faster. Beads of sweat formed along the sides of my face and the back of my neck. Voices blurred in my ears. Suddenly, I bent over and emptied my stomach in the street.

Shakily, I stood up again. The crowd was shifting, moving with Monsieur Dubois and my brother toward the guardhouse. I struggled to follow.

At the entrance doors, two soldiers took Jean-Pierre, who twisted and kicked.

"He's wild!" someone shouted. "Hold him!"

One soldier held him beneath the arms, the other held his legs, and they carried him inside. "Marius!" he cried. "Papa!"

I slumped to the guardhouse steps, just around the corner from where my father was imprisoned below. I put my head in my hands and wept.

Hours passed. As the moon rose higher, ringed with an ominous white haze, the crowd of villagers thinned.

Deep in the night, a small group gathered at the edge of the square and pushed two women, their clothes torn, toward the guardhouse. One held her head high, her face stern. The other pleaded, "I am not a witch! I practice medicine for the benefit of everyone! You've seen me work good, not evil. I am *not* a witch!"

"God will be the judge," said the mercenary.

Sometime in the middle of the night, when the villagers had drifted home, when occasional soft cries and curses rose from the prisoners' cell, I dropped my head across my arms and fell asleep.

Three riders, magnificent knights on horseback, their armor shimmering silver and shields displaying coats-of-arms I had never seen before, thundered into the village square. They threw off their helmets at the feet of the local priest, and displayed bright halos. "We have been sent by God," one said, "to deliver

*your father and brother from wickedness. There will be no trial
here." Each stretched his arms wide and white wings appeared on
his back. Then the leader cried, loud and high-pitched, like a
screeching eagle.*

I woke, trembling, to a painful sound, one that tore at
my heart—the sound of my father's voice, crying out.

I gathered my lute and raced from the steps of the
guardhouse around the corner to my father's cell. "Papa?"
I asked, my hands as cold as the grate I clutched.

An unfamiliar voice answered from the darkness.
"They've taken him—for torture."

"No!" I cried.

"They will get a confession from him, one way or another."

"What will they do?"

"Many things. Tonight they are heating oil."

"For . . . for what?" I asked, though I wasn't sure I
wanted to know the answer.

"They have a funnel. They put it in your mouth and
threaten to pour in burning oil."

I didn't want to believe this. Maybe this prisoner—or
was it a soldier?—was just trying to scare me. "How do
you know this?" I ventured.

"I confessed before they poured. There is no winning,"
the man said, his voice distant, as if he'd already passed
from his body. "If you don't confess, and survive the torture,
you get life in prison, worse than hell itself. Confess and
you get it over with quickly at the stake."

Time passed slowly. I leaned against the building,
knees drawn tightly to my chest, and waited. A cat,

skinny and one ear torn, brushed by my legs, then disappeared.

Merely moments later, Jean-Pierre's dog scooted to my side, body low, cowering, tail wagging. I remembered my brother's words: *he needed a friend.* My own emptiness was so painful that I stretched my hand to him, and he met it in midair with his pink tongue. I patted his thin sides. With small black eyes, he looked straight at me. He leaped up and licked my chin—almost as if he understood—then he settled into a furry ball beside me, bringing a hint of warmth.

Below, metal clanged against metal. Labored breathing joined the sound of footsteps.

"Who's next?" came the voice of the mercenary.

"This one," came a soldier's voice, then a thud. "No, he's already dead."

"You, quick to your feet!"

A whimper, a clink of chains, a shuffle of feet, and the same rotten smell stirred up toward the grate. Then quiet fell as the guard's voice echoed deeper into the building.

"Papa?" I whispered.

"Marius." His voice was weak.

My throat tightened. To hear my father, always so strong and vital, to hear his voice . . . I swallowed and tried to be brave for him. I leaned over the stray dog and grasped the grate. "Papa, what did they do?"

"I confessed," said my father, "to loving my wife and my sons. And that will always be true, but I lied, too. I told them I was a heretic. . . ." His voice trembled. "Only because I couldn't face . . ."

Tears filled my eyes. The dog pushed his nose into my hand, a small comfort.

The other prisoners in the cell seemed to quiet their moans and clinking chains so we could communicate. I fixed a picture of my father in my mind, not below in the cell, but strong and capable in his smithy. He was a tall oak whose leaves were dropping in a fierce wind. And yet he stood, bare as the silhouetted trees on the plateau. I swallowed hard.

"They can take a man's life," my father continued, "but not his soul. Remember that, Marius."

An occasional villager passed by, some swaggering with drink. I didn't care if I was found at the prisoners' grated window. I didn't care anymore about what happened to me. My life and everyone I loved were slipping from me.

"You must save yourself," he said. "Flee to another place and start over. Save your brother and work toward good. Go, please," he said, "before it's too late."

I didn't have the heart to tell my father that Jean-Pierre had been caught. I pulled my lute from its leather case, rested it on my lap, and—offering up the only thing I could—I played.

Beside the grate, with the smell of human waste and rot wafting upward, I played for my father. I strummed until my fingers were numb and my sight blurred with tears. I played also for my brother, alive or dead, somewhere deep within the stone walls of the guardhouse. I played as the moon dropped steadily lower, the sky turned to a dingy blanket of gray, and the sun licked the horizon with hungry orange flames.

THE STAKES

December 24

With the fervor of market day or a Church holiday, the square filled with villagers. Suddenly I remembered. Today *was* a Church holiday. It was Christmas Eve.

Hauling wood planks, several carpenters walked to the platform near the scaffolds and soon began to hammer. Around a sturdy pillar of wood, other workers stacked kindling high.

A horse's hooves clattered across the square. I kept strumming slowly, my mind somehow distant from my fingers. I glanced up. The abbot, heavily robed in black, his fleshy face tinged red, rode his horse toward me, then pulled to a stop in front of me.

"Ah, such music in our midst," said the abbot. "A source of comfort to the people."

I stopped strumming. "Abbot Joseph," I began, trying to keep my voice calm, to hide how much like a worm I felt, cold and squirming before a preying bird. "May I have a word—about my brother and father, both wrongly accused?"

To my surprise, he nodded.

"Come," he said.

Though I was reluctant to leave my father, I rose, my legs stiff and awkward. I'd seize the chance to plead my father and brother's case. It was, indeed, a rare opportunity. To have earned the ear of the abbot—this alone was a miracle. A faint flame of hope lit within me.

Abbot Joseph spun his horse away and headed to the church. Hundreds of years old, it towered above the square. I quickly encased my lute, slung it across my back, and dashed after him.

At the church, a monk led the abbot's horse away. I followed the abbot through the side door before it closed.

Candles burned in the foyer. The abbot's footsteps clattered along the gleaming marble floor. I followed through a passageway, then another, and soon stood in a brightly colored room. Embroidered wool carpets covered the stone floor. A fire burned bright, and warmth poured from the massive hearth.

Colored light flowed through three tall stained-glass windows. One depicted Michael the Archangel, standing with his sword drawn, his foot upon the head of a serpent. The next showed an angel protecting Daniel from the lions in a pit. The third showed a figure robed in white, leading three prisoners from flames, untouched. *My dream!* I was amazed at how similar my dream had been to these images. If only I could hope for a rescue from such heavenly warriors. Sadly, I'd seen such wonders only in the tapestries, glass windows, and sculptures owned by the Church, never in real life.

Seated behind an oak desk, the abbot wrote on scrolls set before him. His chair was high-backed with red velvet cushions framed by ornately carved arms and legs, the only chair in the room. I stood across from him, waiting, hands at my sides.

A monk entered, bowed from his waist, and laid another scroll across the abbot's desk; when the abbot nodded, the monk removed himself to the far corner of the room.

I grasped the edges of my jerkin. Even now, the stakes were being prepared in the square. Maybe the abbot only intended to have me play my lute. I couldn't wait any longer. "My brother and father . . ." I began.

Abbot Joseph held up the palm of his hand and kept his eyes upon the parchment and words scribbled in black ink. "You will wait."

I held my tongue and studied the abbot as he dipped his quill in the inkwell and continued to write. Perhaps he was signing something about the prisoners. Despite Church warnings, despite the dangers, more than anything I wanted to read what was on that paper. *I would learn.* I would find a way to rise above my ignorance. I would find a way to teach myself, if necessary. As my parents had hoped, I would learn to read.

Finally, the abbot set down his quill and met my eyes.

"I can do nothing for your father," he said, the stain on his forehead a deep crimson. He tapped the scroll. "This is a statement from last night's inquiry. Your father confessed to being a heretic. The laws regarding heresy are strict and immovable. To possess heretical literature, to continue in Huguenot thinking, is punishable by death. He will burn at the stake."

"But he's . . ." My throat closed.

The abbot squinted with impatience. "What has been decided is beyond you or me."

I understood. The Church had rules, and even an abbot was subject to a bishop, who was in turn subject to the cardinal, who was subject to the pope himself. And the pope was the very instrument of God.

I forced myself to stand tall. Things were even beyond the abbot's control. I struggled to find my voice. "And what of Jean-Pierre, my brother," I began, my voice faltering, "he's only a child."

The abbot ran his finger along the parchment. "Your brother's fate is not yet sealed. The villagers will tear him apart if he isn't burned at the stake. He cannot stay in Venyre, you must realize that." He paused, glanced at the stained-glass windows, then looked again at me. "If he is truly a *loup garou*, as accused, we will learn that soon enough. These fears"—he dismissed them with a wave of his hand—"prey upon the minds of people. Until we know more about your brother, he could be kept safe at a monastery far from here."

I felt numb. My lower lip trembled. "*M-merci*, Abbot Joseph."

"Not too quickly," said the abbot. He picked up his quill and stroked its long purple feather. "A village is like this," he said, separating the feather with his fingers into a hundred small parts. "When things get out of control, the Church must"—he closed his hand over the feather and smoothed it into one piece again—"make things right. And in many ways, all the churches and villages are like a bird's many feathers working as one—like the Holy Ghost."

"My brother," I blurted. "Then he won't be burned . . . you'll send him away."

The abbot snapped the quill in half. "There is a price."

I waited and held my breath. Waited for the abbot's words to decide my brother's fate.

"There is a price," the abbot repeated, "for your brother's freedom. You think I ask you here for the pleasure of your company?" He laughed to himself. "As Christ said, 'There is no greater love than to lay down one's life for a friend.' The price," he said, "is this: *your life for his.*"

I stood firm, but inside I staggered.

The abbot paused, expressionless. He crossed his arms, sat back in silence, and waited. The church bells began to ring loudly, clanging through the village. "You don't have much time to decide," he said.

The words I could never erase from my mind, my mother's last wishes, my father's plea, now filled my head. *Tell Marius to take good care of his brother.* The bells continued to ring. My answer came quickly, before I could change it out of fear for the flames.

"*Yes,*" I said, "I will trade my life for his at the stake."

Abbot Joseph laughed. "Not the stake. But I see you have a good heart. No, your life will be spent in service to God, playing your lute as a monk, in exchange for your brother's—he will be set free." The abbot rose and adjusted the cap upon his head.

"Music helps us rise above earth's troubles," he whispered. "It is a true gift."

Then he rolled the scroll and handed it to the attending monk. "Take this," he commanded, "and notify Father Arnaud."

THE PRISONERS

I followed the abbot and monk into the bright morning light. From the guardhouse, soldiers led nearly a dozen barefooted people strung together—seven men and five women—to the stake. Ropes circled their necks and fastened their hands behind their backs. Their heads were shaved bare, nicked red in spots. Among them, the two men who had arrived in cages were now walking skeletons.

A few, including my father, had cloth bags of gunpowder tied around their necks, to help the accused die more quickly from explosion and spare them the agony of burning slowly. My father held his head high, neck muscles straining from the weight of the gunpowder. *Marguerite.* She must have found her way to the guardhouse to provide this strange act of kindness.

The mercenary and soldiers shouted at the crowd. "Back up, unless you want to burn along with the others!"

It was just as Brother Gabriel had said. Fear was spreading like grass fire. I hated my own helplessness. What use was a lute on my back against what was happening?

"They'll burn too fast!" a man shouted. "Remove the gunpowder! Dip the heretics from the scaffold! Make them suffer for their sins!"

I felt ill. I had heard of towns where heretics were raised and lowered by ropes, in and out of the flames, as a way to prolong their suffering. God, not here. I could not bear to watch.

Soldiers chained the prisoners to the wooden beam, then hammered the links fast to the post. Facing outward, in a tight circle around the stake, the accused stood quietly. Wood was stacked in long lengths around the base.

From a nearby platform, Abbot Joseph raised his arm. "Villagers of Venyre," he called. "We have nothing to fear. When God is for us, who can be against us?"

My father's voice rang out. "And God is with us! May He forgive you your ignorance, your haughty pride!"

"Silence," commanded Abbot Joseph, "or you will lose your tongue!" He inhaled so sharply that his nostrils pinched, then he continued. "Let the heretics, the workers of sorcery and evil—let them all perish in fires much kinder than the fires of eternal damnation. What mercy is there for those who turn against the Holy Church, the pope, the very heart of God?" Then he read a list of names and their convictions.

"Catherine Perilleau . . . heretic!"

"Michel Cézanne . . . heretic!"

As the rest of the names were read, I pressed through

the crowd, as close as possible toward my father. The rope cut into his neck. His name was read last.

"Emanuel Poyet . . . heretic!"

Crying and cursing filled the air around me.

"Papa!" I cried. "May angels save you! Forgive me, for I cannot!"

My father's eyes, full of deep pain and deep love, met mine.

"Where is the boy? The *loup garou?*" someone shouted.

Just then, a guard came from the guardhouse carrying a small, limp body between outstretched arms toward the abbot. The crowd grew silent and it parted before the guard. I knew in an instant from the dark hair, the fair skin, that the body he carried was Jean-Pierre. "He is dead," said the guard as he approached the abbot.

"The boy," the abbot repeated to the crowd from his platform, "is dead. Sickness—pray it isn't the plague—spreads quickly to the wicked. All the more reason to rid Venyre of such evil."

A murmur went up from the crowd. Villagers began to cross themselves, then cheering filled the air.

"Dead?" I cried, my voice lost amidst the other voices. I rushed toward the guard. The crowd closed in before I could get close enough, but in a glimpse, I saw Jean-Pierre's grayish-white skin, his eyes closed.

Whatever hope remained was trampled within me. *Not my brother. Not Jean-Pierre.*

My chest filled with rage. I lunged, fists clenched, toward the abbot standing on his platform. With a jerk, I was stopped short, yanked back with strong hands and arms. I strained forward, strained against whoever held me. "Let me go!"

"Marius Poyet," the abbot called out over my head, "will redeem his family's wickedness by choosing to dedicate his life in service to God at St. Benedict's."

He gazed down at me; sunlight struck the red birthmark on his forehead. "This day will pass, Marius. Your music, through the years ahead, will be a welcome gift in God's house."

THE FIRE

I twisted around, arm raised to strike whoever held me back. My eyes met Brother Gabriel's, his skin ashen beneath the cowl of his frock.

"They're going to burn my father!" I wailed. "They've killed my brother, and you hold me back?"

"Come," Brother Gabriel said gravely. "I'm here to take you away."

Then he seized my arm, and walked me steadily through the crowd, away from the stake. I struggled to break free and turn back. At the edge of the square my uncle stopped and brought his face to mine.

"Listen!" he said, his forehead gleaming with perspiration. "There is nothing—*nothing*—we can do for your father or your brother now."

"Light the fires!" the mercenary bellowed in the distance.

I turned my head to look as soldiers laid torches to wood around the base of the stake. Then smoke puffed upward, enveloping the prisoners in a gray cloud.

"Papa!" I cried, my heart wrenched from my chest. I fell to my knees. The smell of wood and burning flesh met my nose. I didn't want to breathe any of it in. I groaned like a wounded animal. How could this be happening?

From the crowd rose screams and shouting, cursing and cheering, and pleas for help and pleas for mercy. "Burn the heretics!"

"God help them!"

"Spare them!"

"Let them burn!"

"Mother Mary!"

I clapped my hands over my ears.

Brother Gabriel gripped my shoulder, yanked me to my feet, and forced me to keep moving. "We must leave, right now while everyone is fixed on the fire. If you stay, the crowd will turn on you next. I received your message, but these are fires I cannot put out."

My legs were iron weights, yet they kept me moving away from the stake, past the smithy, and past the shadowed archway, where the dog was lying. He jumped up and trotted alongside as we neared the eastern gate.

So this was the bargain, then, planned ahead of time, that my uncle would lead me back to the monastery to put my life beneath the yoke of a monk's robe. And for what? So I could share my gift of music with a corrupt abbot, the man who had brought on this cruelty, this injustice, who had allowed both my father and my brother to die?

As we stepped outside the gate, the guard who'd

carried my brother strode toward us, empty-handed.

"My brother?" I demanded. "Where did you put him?"

"Ditch beyond the wall. Could be the plague."

I ran ahead to the ditch east of the olive grove. Several steps away from a half dozen other bodies lay Jean-Pierre, face down.

"Marius! Don't touch him. If it's the plague or the sweats, you'll die along with him. I know you love him, but—"

I didn't obey. I flipped my brother over and pushed my head against his small chest. A grief wider and deeper than any cavern I could imagine filled me. I wanted to lie down, to give up completely and die.

Nearby, the dog began to sniff at the corners of a rolled blanket holding a body. "No!" I shouted, and the dog shrank to the ground and withdrew.

In the span of days, my whole world had toppled. What kind of God could do this? I was going crazy, stuck in a nightmare that would not end. I seized my brother by his shoulders and shook him, shook him for dying, shook him hard, shook him until my tears flowed.

"Marius," said my uncle. "Marius, stop."

Something small and gray flew from Jean-Pierre's mouth. The medicine pebble.

Jean-Pierre had obeyed me and placed it beneath his tongue. If only my plan had saved him. I dropped my arms and hung my head.

"Marius," came Brother Gabriel's voice, pressing and urgent. "We have no time. Nothing can be done now. Please trust me."

Suddenly, air wheezed from my brother's lips, then

came an audible filling of his chest. I jumped back. Slowly, slowly, my brother's breathing deepened.

"Brother Gabriel!" I shouted, not taking my gaze from my brother. His amber eyes were fixed in a distant stare, but after a few moments, he blinked. His eyes focused and settled on me.

"Marius," he said, his tongue thick around the word.

I was stunned, unable to speak or move. How could this be? Then I gripped my brother by his shoulders, his body sagging against mine, and held him fast.

"Praises to God!" said Brother Gabriel, tugging at my sleeve. "He's alive. Now, for the love of mercy—"

I couldn't move. Jean-Pierre's heart beat against mine.

"I did what you said," whispered Jean-Pierre. "At the guardhouse . . . the pebble. I was so scared. I didn't know what else to do."

"You did just fine," I said.

I didn't want Jean-Pierre to see the nearby bodies. I held my face close to his. His eyes had shut again.

"Keep your eyes closed," I said, then scooped him up and carried him in my arms like a bundle of rushes. I glanced back at the eastern gate, wondering if Celestin was watching—but no one was there. He, too, must have left his post to watch the burning. I turned toward the monastery. My life lay ahead there—an endless string of predictable gray days. And Jean-Pierre would serve out his life, undoubtedly, in the same way, but at a distant place. At least he was alive.

Brother Gabriel shook his head. "No, Marius. This way," he said, pointing to two donkeys in the distance on the edge of the olive grove. You and your brother must move on, no matter the abbot's orders. Your lives would be at risk if you stayed."

He strode toward the donkeys and I followed, carrying Jean-Pierre, the dog flagging my side.

"Don't look back," I told Jean-Pierre, his arms around my neck. "Don't open your eyes until I tell you."

The donkeys grazed on a patch of dry winter grass. The snow had already melted clear away. Brother Gabriel untied the animals and motioned to the smaller donkey.

"Sit here," I said, setting Jean-Pierre upon the donkey, its winter coat thick and shaggy. "Open your eyes—and hang on."

Jean-Pierre opened his eyes. His skin was pale, but life glimmered in his face. "I've always wanted," he whispered, falling forward and wrapping his arms around the animal's neck, "a donkey."

"We must make haste," my uncle said. "By evening, the abbot will expect to see you at St. Benedict's." He glanced at the sun, nearing its midcrossing of the sky. "He will not send out searchers until tomorrow morning. By then, you will be far away."

"Where's Papa?" Jean-Pierre asked drowsily. Astride the donkey, he wobbled. I steadied him with my hand firmly on his shoulder.

I could not answer. I studied the leather travel pouches our donkey carried. Hunger gnawed at my stomach, but I ignored it.

"Where will we go?" I asked Brother Gabriel, who rode the other donkey, leading us away from the grove.

"To the northeast," he said over his shoulder, "to Huguenot lands, then, if necessary, on to Geneva. To

Switzerland where there is more freedom . . . until the persecution passes. You must live where you can learn to read without being punished."

We had only walked a few paces when I glanced back and stopped. Smoke curled darkly in the sky above the village. It rose and billowed, blacker and blacker, like a beckoning hand hovering in the windless morning. I would not be able to so much as bury my father's ashes, to let him rest beside my mother.

"Marius," Brother Gabriel said, riding back to my side. "We must go quickly, before anyone stops us."

Smoke continued to build and billow. Even now, the abbot was there, presiding over my father's burning. I churned in anger. He had forced me into a bargain over my brother's fate and my own. I spat out my words. "I owe the abbot nothing."

"The best you can do," my uncle said, "is to leave—to move on and become a light in this cursed darkness."

I clenched my teeth, lost in shock as thick as fog.

"And what about Madame Troubène?" I asked. "She's very ill. Who will care for her?"

"I stopped at your home first, looking for you. Marguerite was there. She promised to look after her."

For now, I would lean on my uncle's words. Lean on his strength and move on, though to what, I had no idea.

I tried to absorb a last glimpse of Venyre, its walls built high, meant to keep the enemy out, to provide safety for those within. Today the decree had been carried out to burn the heretics. And tomorrow they would herald the Savior's birth; joyous and festive, villagers would follow the crated lamb through the streets to church.

I would not be there. My family would not be there. Life would never again be the same. I could not take my eyes off the smoke. My father. His image pierced my heart. Tears brimmed. If only I could have saved him. If only I had been a knight with a thousand men, an angel with a legion of angels. But I was only human, only a boy.

No, I was more than that. I was my father's son, on my way to becoming a man.

I filled my chest sharply with air, made the sign of the cross, and adjusted the lute on my back. Flanked by my little brother and a stray dog, I walked away, leaving my life in Venyre behind without another glance back.

A WINTER MOON

We left Venyre farther and farther behind, its windows shuttered tight against December. The Mistral wind howled from the north, quieted for a time, then blew again.

We followed my uncle. The heavy cloak that Brother Gabriel had supplied hung below my breeches and trapped my body's warmth as I walked. Jean-Pierre wore a thick wool blanket around his small frame and hummed as he combed the donkey's wiry mane with his fingers.

I walked silently alongside Jean-Pierre, my hand on his knee. "Where's Papa?" he asked again. "Will he meet with us somewhere, Marius?"

I walked on, unable to answer. The foul smoke of my father's senseless death clung to my clothing, and with each step that took me away, my heart weighted me down. My mind raced back to the past, forward to the unknown, and all the time my feet carried me, almost against my will. I followed the thin, winding road between a patchwork of fields, vineyards, olive groves, and deep forest toward the next village.

Hours later, as we veered onto a sandy path between scraggly cedars, he asked again, perhaps for the twelfth time, "Marius, tell me. Where's Papa?"

I remembered how helpless I had felt the night my brother was born. How certain I was that life could not go on without my mother. And yet it had. Like me, Jean-Pierre would have to pick his way through life as best he could. At least neither of us would be completely alone.

This time, I answered. "He died," I whispered, and my heart tore with the words.

Jean-Pierre looked at me and began to speak, but his small round mouth held no sound.

I squeezed his knee, then placed my hand over my heart. "Papa," I managed, "will be here always. Here with Mama . . . and right beside God."

I still couldn't grasp that my father was gone. He should be in his smithy at the break of dawn, pumping the billows at his forge until the embers glowed a deep red. I would carry his memory forever. At least Jean-Pierre had been spared from witnessing the burning.

I drew the donkey to a stop, reached up, and embraced my brother.

As we traveled, the dog clung to my heels. At a wooden bridge, I reached into my pocket and found the bread I'd intended for my father. I broke off pieces and shared a chunk with Jean-Pierre, then held another piece out in my palm. Gently, the dog lifted the bread from my hand with his soft mouth.

"Good boy," I told him. He jumped clear off the ground and licked my chin.

In the waning light of late afternoon, we paused at a stream and let the donkeys drink. My uncle, Jean-Pierre, and I found a wide, sloping rock, cupped our hands in the icy water, and drank.

Brother Gabriel lifted his face from the stream, water dripping off his chin.

"I have made provisions," he said, walking to the smaller donkey and rummaging through a leather satchel, "for your journey ahead."

"'*Our* journey?'" I asked. I stood up, wiping my mouth with the back of my hand. "Aren't you coming with us?"

He shook his head. "Will we never see you again?" I asked, my voice rising. I couldn't face leaving my only other known relative.

"When you reach the monastery past the next village," he said, reaching into his cloak and withdrawing an embroidered blue scarf and a simple scroll, "you will give this scroll to Brother Etienne, who will send you forward from there. He will send the scarf to me as a sign that you've reached your first resting point."

He turned the scroll to reveal a red wax seal stamped with a cross over a rose, the same rose design on my lute. "You'll travel under the safety of my seal. And we will, I promise, meet soon."

He paused. Jean-Pierre leaned into my side.

"When we near the next village, you'll continue on. I'll

return to the monastery and tell the abbot you fled in the opposite direction."

"But what of you?" I asked. "If the abbot knows that you helped us, won't you be in trouble?"

"The abbot has no power over me," he said, and smiled just enough to deepen his dimples. "I am an equal to him in rank. If changes do not come from good men, the whole Church will indeed rot away. I must stay a while longer. But don't worry. I am not abandoning you."

That night, as stars emerged—faint glimmers of light in the deepening sky—I said good-bye to Brother Gabriel, kissed him on each side of his face, then watched him slip away into the darkness, like an angel leaving for another world.

We continued northeast, Brother Gabriel's scarf and sealed scroll tucked in a leather pouch, and journeyed wide around the walls of the next village. The rising moon illuminated our path.

In a cedar grove, we tied up the donkey and rested close together on soft boughs that we cut and layered on the ground. Wrapped in my cloak, numb with exhaustion, I slept, back to back with my brother.

Hours later, with a start, I woke to the cry of a distant wolf.

Eyes suddenly wide, I lifted my head. The wolf's song drifted eerily on the wind through the woods. *Christmas Eve.* Who knew what might become of us? Our dog lifted his head, too, eyes glinting in the full moon's white beam, and his ears perked up. I sank my fingers into his fur and waited. Somewhere far off, another wolf sang, and two cries melted into one voice, melancholy and piercing.

Then the night again fell silent. Before long, our dog snuggled back into the crook of my arm. I laid down, closed my eyes, and drifted into an uneasy sleep.

In the murky light between night and morning, I awoke. A mist enveloped us. Sweet cedar scented the air. Our dog was curled in a ball, and Jean-Pierre slept soundly with his mouth wide open. I was relieved that the night had passed.

I reached inside my shirt, pulled out the wolf-tooth necklace, and held it in my hand. For a long time, I studied it, felt its sharp point, and turned the last few days over in my mind. My chest was heavy with loss. My whole being ached as I thought of my father. I would honor his life and continue in his brave footsteps, continue toward the dream of reading and learning that he and my mother had shared for me. I would use my mind and trust my heart.

From around my neck, I lifted the leather necklace, then buried it deep beneath our bed of cedar. My courage, from that time on, would come from another place.

I tapped Jean-Pierre's shoulder until he stirred. "We must move on," I said.

With my lute strapped on my back, once again we set off. The sun climbed slowly, steadily upward, burning off the mist, and in the early light a snow-tipped mountain shone ahead, brighter than any spire I had ever seen.

AUTHOR'S NOTE

Though this is a work of fiction, the story of Marius Poyet and his family in mid-sixteenth-century France is historically possible. In France alone in the sixteenth century, thousands and thousands of people—women and children included—were accused of being werewolves; countless numbers of those suspected were put to death at the stake, along with others charged with witchcraft, sorcery, and heresy.

As superstition would have it, a variety of symptoms might indicate that a person was a werewolf. Epilepsy was one sign. A Christmas Eve birth, eyebrows joined above the bridge of one's nose, rough palms (from shaving werewolf fur)—these, too, were indications that one could be a *loup garou*.

The times were brutally difficult. Though the most well-known plague, the Black Death, hit Europe in the late fourteenth century, plagues and illnesses (sleeping sickness, or perhaps influenza, hit France hard in the 1550s) continued to scour the land. Poverty, in part due to overtaxation and financial obligations to the Church, was on the increase, and the level of corruption within the Church leadership had never been higher.

In reaction, Protestantism—a "protest" against the Catholic church—continued to spread. A number of strong religious leaders aided in its growth. Martin Luther's use of the printing press in Germany early in the sixteenth century had much to do with the rapid growth of the Reformation. Lefévre d'Étaples translated the Bible into French and was active in Protestant circles until 1525. In the 1530s John Calvin, a Frenchman, introduced a new form of Protestantism (later to be called Calvinism) that gained increasing popularity with nobles as well as with the laboring class.

Books were expensive and available only to those who could afford them. The most widely translated book was the Bible, which the Church forbade reading on one's own, especially in a language other than Latin. The layperson, or common person, was not trusted to read the Bible on his or her own. Those who could read were suspected of reading materials that ran counter to Church doctrine.

When it came to dissenters of the Catholic faith, the Church and the Crown acted in unison. Indeed, the Catholic church in France, called the Gallican church, followed the king in matters of faith. Because King Henry II knew that books were powerful agents of change, he condemned the printing and distribution of Protestant literature. According to historian Will Durant, "in 1549, France's own King Henry II set himself to crush heresy. By the Edict of Chateaubriand (1551) the printing, sale, or possession of heretical literature was made a major crime, and persistence in Protestant ideas was to be punished with death." Informers were to receive a third of the goods of the condemned.

In response to this censorship, the secret printing of Protestant books and placards (flyers or pamphlets) mushroomed. In France, Protestant believers were called Huguenots, a term derived from the phrase, *le roi Huguet*, the name inhabitants of the city of Tours gave to any ghost seen haunting their city at night. Perhaps the secretive nature of Protestant gatherings led to the sinister name *Huguenot*.

As the Huguenot movement gained a following, pronouncements of heresy increased. For instance, on June 10, 1559, Anne du Bourg, son of a former chancellor, spoke out in the French parliament against the persecutions and said it was "no small thing to condemn those who, amidst the flames, invoke the name of Jesus Christ." In response to his bold words, that following December, he, too, was burned at the stake.

The Catholic Church for centuries had enjoyed absolute political and religous power as the "one Christian church" of Europe. But absolute power can lead to corruption, and the sixteenth century was a time when the Church appeared to be rotting from within. Though there were monasteries, for instance, who did minister to the needy, many other monasteries were run as ruthless baronies, putting an increasing burden upon the population they were meant to serve.

As the Church's influence became weaker, eventually it was forced to address its problems at the Council of Trent, after which many reforms were made to begin to draw the Church back to its basic teachings, especially to the call of service. The Council of Trent, however, also drew up an extensive list of banned books.

Geneva, Switzerland, became a place of refuge for many Huguenots fleeing the persecution of the Catholic Church. In time, however, the strict form of Protestantism encouraged by John Calvin in Geneva led to its own persecutions for those who didn't bend to the ways of the Protestant faith.

Given the challenges of living in the sixteenth century, it is little wonder that music continued to be a great source of comfort, entertainment, and inspiration for peoples of all classes. It is said that fields were filled with the singing of peasants; minstrels traveled from village to village; lords and ladies, even kings and queens, often composed music and played instruments.

The lute was one of the most favored instruments of the day and one of the first to be appreciated as a solo instrument, not just as an accompaniment for vocalists. During the sixteenth century in France, a good musician—such as Marius Poyet—would have readily found an appreciative and grateful audience.

For further reading:

Cohen, Daniel. *Werewolves* (New York, 1996).

Davis, Natalie Zemon. *The Return of Martin Guerre* (Cambridge, Mass., 1983).

Davis, Natalie Zemon. *Society and Culture in Early Modern France: Eight Essays* (Stanford, 1975).

Neuschel, Kristen. *Word of Honor: Interpreting Noble Culture in Sixteenth-Century France* (Ithaca, 1989).

Salmon, J. H. M. *Society in Crisis: France in the Sixteenth Century* (New York, 1975).

For more information:

Visit *Le Poulet Gauche*, a Web site devoted to the history, culture, and daily life of sixteenth-century France at: www.lepg.org

"Legends of the Werewolves" (video documentary). The History Channel, 1998 A&E Television Networks, 126 Fifth Avenue, New York, NY 10011

SELECTED BIBLIOGRAPHY

Baumgartner, Frederick J. *Change and Continuity in the French Episcopate: The Bishops and the Wars of Religion, 1547–1610*. Durham: Duke University Press, 1986.

Berry, W. Grinton, ed. *Foxe's Book of Martyrs*. Tarrytown, N.Y.: Fleming H. Revell Company (first published 1563).

Botting, Douglas, ed. *Wild France*. San Francisco: Sierra Club Books, 1994.

Briggs, Robin. *Early Modern France 1560—1715*. Oxford: Oxford University Press, 1977.

Cohen, Daniel. *Werewolves*. New York: Cobblehill Books, 1996.

Durant, Will. *The Reformation: A History of European Civilization from Wyclif to Calvin: 1300–1564*, New York: Simon and Schuster, 1957.

Lopez, Gary Holstun. *Of Wolves and Men*. New York: Charles Scribner's and Sons, 1978.

Packard, Francis R., M.D. *Life and Times of Ambroise Pare (1510–1590)*. New York: Paul B. Hoeber, 1921.

Pollarde, John. *Wolves and Werewolves*. London: R. Hale, 1964.

Rothrock, George A. *The Huguenots: A Biography of a Minority*. Chicago: Nelson-Hall, 1979.